PRAISE]

C000155944

"Major new voices don
MICHAEL MARSHALL S

"T.E. Grau has that special touch that leaves part of a reader
trapped inside his tales, and that's always a sign that others
should proceed, wide-eyed, into these stories. For me, he's right
up there with the best new generation of horror writers ..."
ADAM NEVILL, author of *Lost Girl*

"T.E. Grau's writing is dynamic and vital and reinforces
the notion that the 2000s and 2010s are a high watermark
in the tradition of horror and the weird."
LAIRD BARRON, author of *Swift to Chase*

"T.E. Grau's odd, edgy stories shine a new light into the dark
corners of human experience. These stories shine with smart
prose, clever—often quirky—insights, and enough weirdness
to make any genre fan froth at the mouth with glee."
GARY MCMAHON, author of *The Concrete Grove*

"Some authors become contemporary favorites of mine
on the merits of only a story or two. Such was the case with
T.E. Grau ... Even as a relative newcomer, he's writing
stories that can stand tall alongside those of much more
established writers of modern weird fiction."
JEFFREY THOMAS, author of *Punktown*

"The shadows evoked by T.E. Grau have teeth,
and they shall endure."
RICHARD GAVIN, author of *Sylvan Dread*

A This Is Horror Publication
www.ThisIsHorror.co.uk

ISBN: 978-1-910471-03-6

First published in 2016 by This Is Horror

Editor-in-Chief: Michael David Wilson
Cover Art: Candice Tripp
Front Cover Design: Ives Hovanessian
Interior Design and Layout: Pye Parr

THEY DON'T COME HOME ANYMORE

A Novella

T.E. GRAU

ABOUT THE AUTHOR

T.E. Grau is an author of horror, crime, and dark fiction whose work has been featured in dozens of anthologies, magazines, literary journals, and audio platforms. His debut book of short stories, *The Nameless Dark: A Collection* was nominated for a 2015 Shirley Jackson Award for Single-Author Collection, and ranks as the bestselling book published by Lethe Press in both 2015 and 2016. Grau lives in Los Angeles with his wife and daughter, and is currently working on his second collection and his first novel.

For Ivy

My Eternal, My Home

"A cage went in search of a bird."
Franz Kafka, The Third Notebook, November 6, 1917

I.

Hettie stood in the doorway, unable to cross the threshold. The sounds coming from within were strange, too coldly official. A low register beep. The whisk of a respirator. There was a smell in the room, something that you would never associate with a seventeen-year-old girl. Not death itself, but what waits for the body afterward.

The room looked massive and the bed small. The girl on the bed smaller still. She was tiny by this point, a good six months into her treatment. A papery husk shoved under a mound of expensive blankets brought from an expensive home. That midnight waterfall of black hair was gone, replaced by mouse brown wisps, like dirty cobwebs caught on the textured white fabric. The sickness had pulled the color right out of it. Hettie couldn't see her face, as the girl's head was turned away from the door. She might have been looking out the window when she fell asleep, into the night sky or the pink glow of magic hour, but a black satin sheet had been tacked up over the window some time ago. Even with its high thread count, it still looked like a cheesy theatre curtain. The girl in the bed obviously didn't want to see what was happening on stage. Or maybe it was to keep out those who had gathered in the parking lot from the first day the news got out. No one was standing out there tonight.

Hettie looked up and down the hallway, wondering where everyone was, even at this hour, considering the status of the girl wasting away inside this room. That she was left alone, even for a minute, was shocking. Outrageous, even. Hettie would never have abandoned her bedside, were she invited in to stand vigil. She would have moved her life into this lifeless room, holding the girl's hand and guarding against anything and anyone who came for her. Even death itself. She would have brought flowers—hydrangeas, most likely, white and fluffy like snow cones—and books to read aloud. She would sing to the girl buried under the blankets, and wait for her eyes to open and recognition to come. They would be together, breathing the same sanitized air, accustomed then to the other odors just underneath, dreaming as one when sleep came for both.

But the unclaimed parts of the hospital remained empty and quiet. It was late, slipping toward early morning, and no one stirred in room or corridor, aside from the woman moaning several doors down, her voice rising and falling in that same steady rhythm of the heart monitor and respirator flanking the girl in the bed. It was almost musical. She had continued this refrain for almost an hour, which was as long as Hettie had been standing in the doorway, watching the rise and fall of those blankets, her mind sketching out what was beneath them, colored in by years of memory and a thousand study hall fantasies. She listened to the unbroken meter of the machines keeping Avery Valancourt alive.

Just walk into the room. Go to her. It's so simple. What are you afraid of? The silence between the mechanical sounds felt suffocating, aggressively condescending, daring her to step up and get knocked down. Hettie knew that if she moved she'd break the spell, and something terrible would happen.

Without a ding, an elevator door rumbled open somewhere on the same floor. It was impossible to tell from which direction the sound came. She couldn't hear the footsteps but was certain they were there, heading in her direction. The girl had been left alone too long, and now someone was coming. Hettie had to make her move. Now or never. She gathered her strength, raised her foot, and stepped into the room.

II.

It happened during fifth period AP physics. As with all of Hettie's classes—except for trigonometry, oddly enough—Avery wasn't in this class, and she would have already checked out of scholastic endeavors for the day. In the fall and winter, she would have been at cheerleading practice. Or show choir if it was spring. But she dropped out of both. She dropped out of everything, showing up each morning later and later, but still arriving, to make her appearance. Not for social reasons, it turned out, but to keep the school from getting her mother involved in the rapidly growing and difficult to conceal situation in which she found herself. Avery's father was contacted via e-mail, as he didn't live in town anymore, staying present in his only daughter's life through sizable "school supply" checks, and the occasional Skype session when he was drunk and feeling paternal guilt.

Avery's near complete withdrawal from the school that she once ruled with a disinterested hand sent her fiefdom into a spiral of anxious confusion, throwing the entire construct off-kilter. It was as if the brightest bulb of a neon store sign had gone out, leaving the whole text unreadable, the establishment meaningless and therefore irrelevant to passers-by. School dances were poorly attended. Fights broke out amongst long-standing friends. The janitor quit. Even the football team stumbled, choking away an easy third-quarter lead in the state play-offs to a far outmatched foe. The starting middle linebacker didn't bother to show up for the game. He had dated Avery for two weeks through love notes in seventh grade.

The administration was finally forced to take action, even at the risk of social impropriety. A report sent to the Valancourt home from the school guidance counselor expressed that Avery was "becoming distant" in her interactions with her friends and teachers, and that she seemed "disconnected" from her usual social and civic activities which had been so carefully curated from an early age to give her maximum exposure in the present, and every benefit later in life. The abandonment of this life plan was baffling to the faculty, and was the topic of cheap coffee conversation not just in the teachers' lounge, but across many dinner tables throughout town.

The kids in the school weren't so circumspect in their appraisal of Avery's strange behavior. The smear campaigns started right away, siege engines hitting the ground full-grown and vicious, with factions circling like greedy vultures, eager to tear down the hero they had built up since kindergarten. Rumors cropped up by the hour, branching off of previous speculation, folding several in on themselves and morphing into something entirely different, but sharing the same core DNA that Avery was secretly a horrible person and everyone knew it all along. Drugs, some said. *Heavy* drugs, like the kind you buy from black people downtown. An abusive boyfriend, who was often tied into said heavy drugs and the black people downtown. AIDS seemed to burn hot the longest, as it contained all of the previous elements of drugs and black people, and it was fatal to boot. Perfect. It also best explained the curious bruises her close girlfriends, and a no-nonsense gym teacher, said they saw on her body. The fatigue, the depression, the unnamed pills she supposedly carried around in the Tic Tac box stowed inside a zippered pocket of her Hermès handbag. The slow but inexorable draining of who Avery Valancourt had once been, replacing her with something altogether different, like a bleached-out clone.

But Hettie didn't care about any of these things. Rumors. The changes. All she knew was that Avery had spoken to her, and what she said had changed Hettie's life.

"You going to tell on me?"

Avery phrased the words as a weary question, but it came across more like a dare. Or maybe a secret pact stated with a guarantee of complicity.

Hettie stood bolt upright, trying to process the scene in which she now found herself while Avery smoked a cigarette on the one toilet in The Weeds. This was the name given to the furthest flung bathroom in the school, squeezed between the boiler room and the back emergency exit as if built in a hurry to satisfy some antiquated building code regulating the secret ratio of student enrollment and corresponding toilets. The filthy interior, scrawled with bootleg gang slogans, poorly rendered caricatures of genitals captioned with specific student names, and every wall polka-dotted with cigarette burns and fist-size dents, was hidden away from the cleanliness of the school at large by a nondescript door. Outside of smokers and amateur graffiti artists, it was never used by any God- or microbe-fearing student or teacher or sentient biped other than Hettie, who had 'privacy issues' when she needed to perform certain necessities in the bathroom, and so always slunk her way to The Weeds. She had tried to train her insides to only have to go in the morning or at night in the safe confines of her home, and it usually worked. But today it happened in physics, and was a situation that couldn't wait two more hours, so she asked for a hall pass and headed out past the lockers, the vending machines and the gym, and made her way to The Weeds, looking behind her the whole way. No one showed any interest in where she was going. No one ever did.

When she arrived at the door, she didn't even think to knock, which is how she discovered Avery Valancourt sitting on the toilet, legs sprawled out in front of her, not bent and dainty and balanced on tiptoes like one would imagine. Her cigarette was mostly gone, but Hettie could tell by the filter that it was one of those long ones. The sort of cigarette that you smoke when you really enjoy smoking.

Avery just sat there, waiting for Hettie to answer her question that really wasn't one. This was the first Hettie had looked straight at her since they were kids, without Avery talking to a friend, smiling at a hallway compliment or rolling her eyes to the ceiling. Even in her present state of physical disrepair, her features had bloomed somehow. Were more alive and luscious, like a show rose at the very peak of maturity, moments before it begins to lose its first petal. Under all that velvet, a certain hardness had crept around her eyes, but that didn't detract from her unusual beauty. If anything, it enhanced it. Made it more mature and dangerous to the bland bowls of lukewarm oatmeal that surrounded her every day. Avery Valancourt didn't seem like she was from this town, or even this part of the world. But through a series of unforeseen events and the existence of a condemned bathroom, she now sat low in front of Hettie, $300 jeans pulled down to her ankles, and waited for Hettie to answer her question and enter into a private confidence. She even arched an eyebrow, like a Disney villain.

Hettie felt her feet turning in. Her knees buckling. She didn't know if it was because she had to go to the bathroom, or because she felt like she would fall over at any moment.

"N-n-no. Of course not," Hettie stammered, her mouth suddenly very dry. There was no sink in The Weeds, which was another one of its repellent charms. "Yeah, right," Avery said, and took a deep drag off her cigarette, letting the smoke leak slowly out of her nose like a dragon without any breath left in its body. Hettie had never seen anything so amazing. "You're all a bunch of fucking hens."

"I'd *never*," Hettie said, and meant it with every fiber of her being, unconsciously moving forward a step to emphasize her vow. "Never *ever*."

Avery looked at Hettie for a long time, her perfectly shaped eyes expressionless, bouncing back the deep emotion flushing Hettie's cheeks. She blinked several times, as if trying to unstick a microfiche scan back though the pictures of her mind, looking for a visual match to this unremarkable girl standing in front of her, that had shared the same grade and succession of bigger and better funded schools with her for the last eleven years but never registered an imprint on her personal lifetime yearbook.

Avery lowered her eyes, rubbing the front of her forehead with her fingertips. "You might be the only friend I've got."

A thunderclap went off in Hettie's brain, flattening everything behind. That was it. That was all Hettie needed to hear for the rest of her life. Any future words that supposedly had meaning, any congratulations, loving sentiments, any marriage proposals, job offers, or lottery winnings, would pale in comparison to those eight words. Nine, if you count "I've" as "I have," which Hettie most certainly did not. People didn't talk that way. Avery most certainly didn't talk that way, especially when she was talking to Hettie, which is exactly what she did that afternoon at 2:16 in The Weeds, naming her as a friend. And not just any friend, but her one and only.

Fifteen minutes later, Avery collapsed in the parking lot, and was rushed to the hospital, nearly dying on the way. Some say she did die en route and was saved by EMT heroism, but that could have been just another rumor. Death always makes the best stories.

III.

Find a safe place to die, the man with the glasses had said. *And make sure it is away from the people and away from the sky.*

Hettie recalled that the man didn't use contractions, speaking as if he had learned English from precisely translated American television that didn't exist. Or maybe reading too many bad novels written by frustrated academics who knew the language but not how to use it, filling self-pubbed books from cover to cover with stilted dialogue that had no music. *This is the time of the Becoming. You only have a few hours left.*

Dressed in an expensive party dress that bunched and gaped in all the wrong places, Hettie slowly dragged the high heels chewing up her feet deeper into the city's industrial zone, heading for the canals. She needed to get into the sewer system and wasn't strong enough to lift the cast iron manhole covers. She was hoping to find a missing one on her way, imagining herself scuttling down into the cool darkness like a shiny green beetle, but apparently the scrap metal thieves in this part of town were too lazy. Perhaps they were all dying like Hettie was and couldn't spare the effort.

She clutched a red backpack to her chest like a floatation device as she pitched and staggered on the brutal heels, trying to stay on the sidewalk and not spill out into the empty streets that ran like mercury moats, eager to swallow an outlander. Boarded-up store fronts, machine shops, and small factory spaces that once made things that this country couldn't remember, crowded in over the gum-spotted pavement. Faded signs. Corner diners that fueled a different era chased out of the American Dream by torch-bearing misers willing to trade the future of the United States for two dollar socks and ten thousand dollar automobiles. Cheap graffiti that was as bored as it was crude covered everything. All going through the motions of workaday degeneration. Every unguarded pane of glass was broken, leaving blackshot eyes staring at the teenage girl struggling on the cement in her stolen commencement dress, walking like a toddler that just discovered its legs, or more rightly, a person that was very old, and shrugging off the use of every limb. She had to get deeper into the city, to the edge, where she could hide her body.

If you die out in the open, before you are ready, they will find you and take you away.

At long last, the air took on the stench of rot, detectable even through the medicinal numbness of her sinuses. Hettie was hoping the smell wasn't her. The fishy, fecal undertone reassured her that it was geographic in origin, and that she was close to the canals that took out waste fluids from the hemorrhaging city and brought in salt water to hopefully wash it away clean. By the odor in the air and the black mold that seemed to crawl from every cracked thing that touched the ground, the ocean wasn't doing its part.

Her joints ached and her bones hurt. The unfamiliar clothes felt like sandpaper, overpriced fabrics chaffing her dry skin. Every step felt like she had nails hammered into the balls of her feet, and the wound on her inner thigh bowed out her legs, throwing off her already destroyed sense of balance. Her head was on fire, but when she touched her forehead, the skin was icy cold. She could taste nothing in her mouth except the taste of nothing in her mouth. Had anyone noticed, they would have suspected the flu, brought on by the stress of the last two weeks, which were clearly the most stressful in all of her sixteen years. But no one noticed, allowing her to come to the realization that she wasn't just sick, she was *infected*. She knew that it was real. That it had *worked*. What the man with the glasses had warned her about. What the thing that lived in the tall building had promised. But Hettie still had a hard time processing this new reality, even as she was gripped ever tighter by the physical realization of it. The truth was unfurling inside her, marching on tiny legs into every cell of her body. Death was coming, and then something else was coming after that.

You will wake up on a table, being cut apart. Your sentient pieces stored in jars, zipped into bags. Burned. Or perhaps something worse ...

She arrived at a chain railing overlooking a channel choked with refuse, and picked her way down the cement stairs built into the tide wall, her legs shaking like a palsy victim. She was losing control of her body. It was slipping from her, tamped down by those tiny feet, with a promise to be returned at a later date, changed in ways that were irreparable. How long? How long would she be down here, dying and waiting? The man with the glasses never told her. She hadn't even thought to ask.

Your new eyes will open inside a wooden box, and you will not be strong enough to break free. Not without feeding. You will be entombed inside the earth, waiting for an end that will never come.

At the bottom of the staircase a cement landing fronted six round openings that burrowed back into the city, each surrounded by three rings of red brick-like lips circling a mouth. A lamprey clamped onto the metropolitan underbelly, if parasitic fish wore strawberry red lipstick. Slimy water dribbled out of the lamprey's mouth and into the brackish canal stream. The smell was overwhelming. This entire drainage system built two centuries ago was declared a federal Superfund site last year, and still nothing had been done to what was deemed "one of the country's most polluted urban waterways" by the perfectly coifed news anchor while Hettie's parents just shook their heads. The term 'polluted' was generous, and probably should have been replaced with 'lethally toxic.' Either way, Hettie's parents were outraged into doing nothing.

So choose wisely and plan accordingly, as a mother would with a child. Prepare your bed, secure your tools, and memorize your route.

Hettie removed her shoes and put them into the backpack, feeling like she was moving in slow motion, because she was. Slinging the pack over her shoulder with difficulty, she bent down and crawled into the lamprey's mouth head first, her knees scuffing and bleeding on the broken glass, rotting sticks, and chewed-up pieces of the city. She didn't feel it. Even if she did, she wouldn't have cared. What would have been the worst thing to happen? It would kill her?

When you wake up, you will be the reborn dead. Like an infant, you will need to practice everything. Everything.

As Hettie moved through the wet, the blackness around her started to lighten in the back of her eyes. She could see details of the walls, things flitting in front of her. She could hear the life in the tunnel, and the earth which surrounded it. Chewing mouths, beating hearts, and the electrical fizz of a million brains firing their own private synapse diaries. For a moment, she wasn't sure if she was listening to herself and the stew of a trillion organisms that swam inside the skin sack covering her fluids. She was aware of it all inside her. Heard them speaking to each other, speaking to her. The line between the self and the outer was becoming hazy. But that could just be the creep of death, following the breadcrumb boulders she had set along the trail.

A scraping sound came from behind her, and she stopped, thinking briefly of a book she had read, years ago when she was younger. It was becoming difficult to remember things now, numb as she was amid this noise.

Memories were draining away like sand, flowing out the bottom of her feet and disappearing into the ocean far behind her. But this one, this book, stayed afloat, at least for a second. It was about a clown who hid in the sewer, holding colorful balloons and waiting to kill anyone who came too close. Children, gay men, anyone. *It*, the book was called, written by a King. She remembered it scaring her, making her terrified of dark tunnels that waited underground, and the things that might lurk there. She had heard all of the stories about alligators and albinos and mole people who all seemed to live in harmony down below. A whole new subclass had moved underneath Las Vegas after the last economic crash. She now found herself hoping that she'd run into one or all of these things, even that chuckling clown, because she knew she would be hungry soon. And she wouldn't be afraid anymore. "Everything floats down here." No, not everything. Some things sink.

Listen to your instincts, and practice.

A hiss issued from somewhere in front of her. Her eyes cut through the dark and she spotted it immediately. A possum, balled up in a filthy side tunnel, glaring at her with bristling malice, all pink and grey and needle teeth. Possibly the world's ugliest animal looked even more loathsome down under the ground, like burying it turned it into something else. She would remember the spot for later, after it was over. Right now, she needed to vomit, and did, heaving up something wet and reddish black from her disintegrating insides.

Practice makes perfect. Practice makes perfect.

IV.

Hettie arrived home minutes after the ambulance left the school parking lot. She sprinted from the scene and didn't stop until her left bare foot (she had lost her shoe several blocks previous) slapped on the flagstone of the entry walk to her house.

Inside, she ran up the stairs, shedding outerwear as she went and stomping her feet into the brown shag covering each step. Reaching the top, she trudged down the hall and dove into her room, landing face down on the bed. The thick comforter absorbed most of her sobs, but not all of her screams.

"What the dickens?" Hettie's mother Hilde, a tall, thick-boned woman with tall, thick framed glasses and a Prince Valiant bob, appeared in the doorway, wiping oil paint off her fingers with a stained t-shirt rag. "What's all the racket?"

Hettie didn't raise her face from the bedding. "Oh, mom, it's horrible. *Horrible!*"

Hilde padded over to the bed in suede clogs, covering the woolen socks pulled up high on calves lightly haired and knotted like an oak branch. "What is?"

"It's the end ... It's *over!*"

"What happened, for goodness sake?"

"She fell down. She ... She ... She's going to die, I just know it."

"Who? *Who?*"

"Avery ... Avery's going to die."

Her mother paused, shoulders slumping as the crisis amped down sharply. "Is this another one of your friends? Those 'school-only' friends of yours? The ones you never bring around here because you're ashamed of your family?"

Hettie began crying harder, a wail clipping off at the end as she devolved into that paralyzed, choking inhale, midway between hyperventilation and a chronic case of the hiccups.

"Calm it down, now. You're going to have a conniption."

"I—don't—care."

"You better care. Your great uncle Friedrich died of agitation. About those two horses and the crabapple tree. It's a real concern, Henrietta."

"You don't—understand. If she dies—I will too."

"Don't be so dramatic. You have lots of friends. I hear you talking to them on the phone all the time."

Hettie's breathing was stubbornly returning to normal, even at the mention of those phone calls to people who most certainly wouldn't be considered 'friends' by any stretch of the imagination. "But she—was special. She was the best one. Of all the girls, she's always been the best."

"They'll be others. And if not?" She made a clicking sound out of the side of her mouth. "Your father and I don't talk to one person we went to high school with."

"You and dad don't have *any* friends."

"We sure do," she said, putting indignant hands on hips. "We have each other. What else would a person need?"

"I need *her*. I need Avery. And she needs me, too, mom. She needs me to keep her secret."

"Oh, goodness grapes ..." Hettie's mother stood up, clearly uncomfortable to the point of irritation. "Girls and their secrets."

"There's something wrong with her. I'm going to help."

"Help your mother first by taking your laundry to the basement and throwing in a few loads. It looks like a tornado hit this place."

A short time later, down in the hushed stillness of the partially finished basement, amid the cobwebs and exposed beams and boxed-up memories, Hettie stood in front of the washing machine, a mountain of dirty clothes at her feet, the washer chugging and sloshing, and stared up into the one tiny window letting in the last rays of that day's sun. She pushed her energy, her presence, out through the window and up into the sky she couldn't see. She told it to find Avery in the hospital, and to stay there with her, protecting her, until she could properly arrive.

V.

It was Saturday morning, which meant that Hettie's parents were at the Midtown Farmers Market, drinking small batch coffee and discussing the merits of locally grown boysenberries while filling their yaps with sweatshop raspberry jam. They left Hettie alone, as they had since she was very little, preferring to raise a self-sufficient child than one who was programmed to be a slave to taskmasters. This seemed to be a Machiavellian answer to a softball question, dropping an innocent into Darwin's testing pool and rowing the boat away. But if a child actually made it into adulthood without being kidnapped, raped, and/or murdered, they'd probably be pretty independent and self-sufficient. Self-starters. They'd probably also have missed out on a lot of parenting, not to mention a good portion of normal childhood innocence.

Hettie made a few of her phone calls while preparing herself a breakfast, then took her tea (English Breakfast—her mother's Earl Grey was a perfumey nightmare) into her parents' bathroom. Her mother never wore a stitch of makeup, declaring it the cruel dictum of misogynists and self-loathers, but she kept a few of the basics in a small black makeup case stored behind the pipes under the sink. Hettie's Auntie Viola had brought it over on her one and only visit to the house, and attempted to do a makeover on her sister. That hadn't ended so well, with tears and accusations left festering for twenty years, and Hettie never saw her again. Auntie Viola drank a lot. And wore a lot of makeup. Her mother had said those were never a very good combination, self-loathing or not.

With a bit of maneuvering, Hettie pulled the makeup bag from under the sink, shook the dust off into the toilet, and unzipped it. There was a dark maroon lipstick, crusted over with age. A mascara that was totally dry, and a four color eye shadow compact. Hettie would use all four.

VI.

The front doors of the hospital slid open and Hettie stepped through. The doors closed quickly behind her, nearly clipping her backside, drowning out the songs and chants of the boisterous vigil that had collected in the parking lot moments after the news vans arrived two days ago.

Her face was done up in five shades of loud colors that perched on her skin rather than blending in with it. Dark purple lips. Bright blue eye shadow accented with lines of yellow and green. Cheeks covered in red blush that brought to mind the word 'rouge.' She wore a dress made of some long outlawed fabric that belonged to her grandmother, that was last used as a costume, high heels two sizes too large, and a wide-brimmed woman's hat that her mother had employed as a base for some sort of bird diorama. Hettie looked bold. She looked ridiculous. She looked like she was wearing an absurd disguise straight out of a '70s British sitcom instead of a well-to-do member of the Valancourt clan.

All eyes turned to look at her. Nurses, orderlies, news producers, walk-ins, fretting family members of any of the hundreds of patients housed in this factory of blind hope. There was a dip in the noise, and after a split second of non-recognition, they all went back to their phones and conversations and worries.

Hettie walked through the intake reception and headed for the nearest hallway into the hospital proper. She didn't know where she was going, but made sure she walked with purpose anyway, following the old axiom that if you acted like you belonged somewhere, no one would question if you actually did. Tell yourself that you're a rock star, and you'll *be* a rock star. The article she had read about this was published in one of those men's magazines with half naked starlets on the cover ("being brave") and way too many cologne ads, and focused on getting into A-list nightclubs, but she figured it would work anywhere. Confidence pumped to the level of giving zero fucks was portable, at least in theory.

"Excuse me," a voice said from behind Hettie, who walked on, prepared for this initial interference but having trouble keeping her balance in those wretched heels that made her move like a drunk person, no matter how hard she gripped her toes, or high she held her chin.

"*Excuse* me," the woman repeated, more forcefully. Hettie snapped her fingers to a silent beat like she was listening to headphones somewhere under that hat. "Stop!"

Hettie did, then turned slowly and held a gloved hand to her chest like she'd seen women do in old movies. "Are you speaking to me?" she asked, affecting a continental accent and trying to bat her heavy lashes but only succeeding in sticking them together, turning her demur flutter into Morse code.

"Where are you going?" the nurse said. She was a thick woman with Q-tip hair and a permanent furrow carved into her brow. In short, she was straight out of Central Casting for 'No-Nonsense Intake Nurse.'

"To visit young Ms. Valancourt," Hettie said, dabbing at her protesting eyes that were starting to water. Perfect timing.

"No you're not," she said, clipboard at the ready position and cocking her pen. "Visitation is restricted to all but essential family."

"I'm her sister."

She tapped the clipboard. "No siblings listed. So, unless you're her mother or her recently reassigned father, you need to get in line with the rest and go through the family attorney if you want to set up a visit."

The nurse walked forward and handed her a business card. She must have had a stack of them hidden in one of her many pockets. The card was thick, gold embossed font printed on expensive card stock. *Sy Katz*, it read. *Esquire.*

Hettie hobbled out of the hospital. She pulled off her hat and smoothed her sweaty hair that was teased and crimped through three different decades. She looked past the mob milling about in the parking lot and up into the sky that had turned grey while she was inside, searching for the sun. It was nowhere to be found. What she did see was a single engine prop plane arcing across the sky without a sound, towing a sky banner that read "GET WELL SOON, AVERY! WE ♥ YOU!—VIC'S MARKET."

Honking came from the access driveway into the lot. A fleet of food trucks were pulling in. Excited chatter began as everyone rushed toward the trucks, surging with the syncopated movements of a bird flock. The chorus of an insufferable dance track blared suddenly from huge speakers, as the local pop radio station finished setting up a booth and was now live on air. Several girls, and a few boys started dancing, snapping selfies in between beats.

This wasn't public grief, support for a dying teenage girl. It was a circus, being fed in tiny bites to the gaping maw of social media.

As Hettie tried to process the impromptu block party that had spontaneously—or maybe quite purposely—cropped up in the parking lot of St. Vincent's Hospital, two girls, both of them two grades behind Hettie, walked up quickly and leaned against a nearby lamp post as if ordered there, wearing nearly identical sophomore year outfits down to the pink flip-flops and identical side ponytails. One of them was eating blue cotton candy, picking through it with a disgusted look on her face, lips curled up over braces that gleamed in the weirdly bright grey light. The other held up her Starbucks cup like it was an ID badge. Probably was.

"I'll bet she's totally faking the leukemia," said cotton candy. "Like, who would put *that* out there?"

"It's so not a good look," Starbucks said, looking back and forth while attempting to appear casual, like she was waiting for someone to ask her to dance.

"I mean, blood cancer, or whatever? Like, who even knows what leukemia *is* anymore, right?"

"*Ew.*"

"I'll bet all of her hair falls out."

"She wears extensions anyway."

"Those will probably fall out, too. And her eyebrows."

"*Ew.*"

Cotton candy raised one long, thin leg into the air in front of her. "I wish my legs had leukemia. I'd never have to shave again."

"Right?"

It went on and on like this, as they picked through cotton candy and held up coffee cups they weren't drinking out of and figured out seventy-four ways to say the same thing, but that one word echoed out from inside the lawnmower engine noise of dumb girl chatter: Leukemia. Avery had leukemia. *Blood cancer*, is how she put it. This could have been just another rumor, but for some reason, the news hit Hettie in the lower part of her stomach, where she often weighed out truth from lies, and hid her many, many secrets. Leukemia. Blood cancer. Kiddie cancer. Usually fatal.

Hettie literally, and figuratively, fell out of her shoes, dropping down at the feet of the walking girls, on hands and knees, as if in supplication.

Cotton candy's sneer widened, taking in the entire left side of her face. Plasticine blue was woven into her metallic teeth.

"Who are you dressed as, some old lady's mom?"

"*Ew.*"

VII.

Hettie sat in the hallway next to the door of her parents' bedroom. Behind the wall came the sounds of vigorous sexual congress, spiced up by little snips of doggie noises. Yips and tiny barks. Playful growls and panting. Her parents had an almost embarrassingly robust sex life, and she was neither disgusted nor titillated by the goings on a few feet away, separated by a thin layer of wood, insulation, drywall and paint. She wasn't even interested. She was merely waiting.

The culmination came at last (without a howl, thank God), followed by the wind down, and then the satisfied small talk. Planning out the events of the next day. Grocery lists. Hettie checked her watch. Four minutes left and they'd both be snoring, neither bothered by the other. They were a perfect pair, those two.

Five minutes later, Hettie was back in her room, where she emptied a bag of cell phones onto the floor. There must have been nearly a dozen, but she never kept count. She picked through a few random flip phones until she found one that was wider and taller. A smartphone. Her parents just laughed at her over their plates of gluten-free spinach tortellini when she brought up getting a cell phone the day after her sixteenth birthday.

"We have a perfectly good phone that plugs right into the wall," her mother had said, making that face with the shake of the head that always made her look like a Muppet.

Hettie looked at her dad, a nearly translucent man with hair just a shade whiter than his skin. He shrugged, the same way he did when discussing the injustice of capitalism while opening the financial page in the newspaper to check his diversified portfolio. "The First Tribes used smoke signals to communicate."

She wasn't sure if he was joking, or was actually suggesting that she light fires whenever she wanted to make a personal call on something other than a landline. She never knew when he was joking, because he always said the weirdest shit, and never laughed. He'd smile and open his mouth like he was going to laugh, but no sound ever came out. People always assumed that he'd laughed at their story or joke, but he never did, mastering the art of inferring a laugh without making a sound. He was a hit at parties, and people always went away thinking they had been so charming.

Hettie turned on the iPhone, waited for it to load, then pulled up a search engine. She typed "leukemia" with an inexpert finger, then tacked on "chance of death." After a few minutes of reading, she didn't want to continue. What did the fucking internet know anyway?

VIII.

Days passed. Weeks, vaguely marked by the holiday breaks that arrived so frequently after Halloween. She hated holiday vacations, because it meant she'd be home, with her parents in their cluttered house, but most importantly, away from school, and the daily reality show she shot inside her head that starred Avery Valancourt. But this year, the vacations mashed together with each day spent at school. Hettie couldn't tell any of the holidays apart, as she was moving about in a daze. Every part of her that meant anything was miles across town, looking for a way to get inside and set up a new home.

Avery had slipped into a coma two days after being admitted into the hospital. If only Hettie had found a better way in to see her before she drifted away into herself. If only Avery could have seen that she was there for her, at her bedside, keeping away the riffraff while putting all of her positive energy toward her recovery. She'd pray her special prayers and will her back to health, and then they could take up their friendship first kindled in The Weeds. Avery would grow strong, as would their bond, and all would be right with the universe, just as high school ended and the rest of their lives together would begin, without any of the strictures of childish cliques and clueless parents. The reality show would become a documentary, one of those grand IFC affairs shot by an over-earnest hipster who would understand the beauty of their unique relationship, and the critics would drop to their knees in praise. If only she could get in. Hettie prayed for a sudden heart attack or death by a pack of wild dogs in the future of one Sy Katz, Esquire.

Comatose teenagers apparently don't have the same sizzle as those fully conscious and visibly suffering. Once the local news announced the coma, the parking lot block party quickly unraveled. Vigils burned their candles down to the foil and no one fetched new ones. No more chatty airplanes in the sky. Everyone went home and looked for the next distraction, while a girl wasted away on the fifth floor of St. Vincent's, guarded by a specially compensated hospital staff with strict orders to let no one in.

The quick spread of community apathy was no different at school. The wall of posters and collages, many of them made on assignment in art class, stopped growing, then went into reverse. The taped snapshots of Avery goofing off between classes or leading a cheer lost their adhesion and began to fall, ending up crooked, dangling, or on the floor. Naturally, it wasn't long before these photos were defaced, and not just by the boys, and not just by the students. Beards were drawn on Avery's perfect skin. Cigarettes sticking out of her pouty mouth. Pubic hair where it didn't belong. Crudely formed phalluses zooming into her pouty mouth, staccatos of fluid leading the way. The administration issued a school-wide memorandum warning against such acts of vandalism, vowing to keep the *Tribute Wall to Our Avery* up until she came home. But the threat seemed half-hearted, the sentiment forced. The students felt it, and were soon ripping down whole portions of the posters. Someone smeared shit—actual feces—across a lower portion of a pink and silver addition created by the freshman class. It was then that the principal decided to take it all down, making yet another promise to redo the whole tribute if and when Avery was released from the hospital and returned to school. Everyone knew that wasn't going to happen, including the principal. Physical copies of the candid photos that her friends had supplied for the posters started popping up in the most inappropriate places, like under the sanitation cakes in the urinals. Some enterprising weirdo put up a set of fifteen good to near-mint "Avery Valancourt Tribute Photographs" for sale on eBay, advertising them as part of something called the *Sick Teen Superstar* series, but by then, no one cared enough to make a bid. The auction came and went, and the page disappeared. The deification was over. A god had died in its sleep, and now everyone was back to staring at themselves.

Hettie was having the opposite reaction. She moved through school like the ghost she always was, feeling less connected to the physical world around her than usual, going more undetected than ever. No one knew her bond with Avery, or that Hettie was probably the last person she had spoken to at the school before being hauled away in the ambulance to be locked up in a stucco tower like some fairytale princess.

Hettie's grades suffered, which put in jeopardy her scholarship to the local tiny, overly precious liberal arts university her parents had selected for her when she had declared no interest in selecting a college. Her parents were angry, but only with the high school administration for not properly allowing a child to express her grief, and not properly counseling any of the students throughout the whole Avery Valancourt ordeal. They had never met her, nor seen her outside of the news stories, the billboards, and the citywide tribute concerts, but on instinct ruled against anything that related to public schooling, which they saw as beholden to nefarious special interests that certainly didn't have the best interests of their child in mind. Hettie remembered her father crying for three days straight when she was in the third grade after his promotion at work never came through, meaning he wouldn't be able to send her to private school. The sound of his sobs as he faced down his failure alone in the upstairs bathroom still embarrassed her to this day.

One morning Hettie decided to stop going to school, and made it known to the adults in her life that she wouldn't be going back. Her parents rallied. "Depression" was whispered, and PTSD was debated with the same vigor as if this seventeen-year-old girl had just returned from a tour of Islamabad. Finally, due to the circumstances, Hettie's test scores, and previous GPA up to the day Avery fell ill, and on recommendation from the school district's own psychologist, Hettie was allowed to graduate early. She would spend the rest of the year completing her remaining coursework as 'independent study,' and waiting out the next phase of her life, away from the turmoil of high school, and all those daguerreotype ghosts of things that happened there. It would be the best for everyone, it was decided, especially with the news that leaked out and went viral that Avery probably wouldn't survive the week. The chemo wasn't working, her body wasn't responding to any treatment. Hettie was right that first day. Avery wasn't just sick. She was dying.

IX.

Hettie felt like she was creeping, taking the exaggerated cartoon steps of a mustachioed villain meant to maximize stealth, but she was only just walking, albeit slowly, until she came to a stop at the far end of a painfully manicured lawn that must have taken up the better part of an acre. The remains of what was probably hundreds of bouquets and several dozen live news broadcasts littered the rectangle of grass on the street side of the sidewalk. The Valancourt lawn, however, was immaculate, cut short and uniform like the new rubberized turf installed on the school football field. A green so vibrant it hurt the eyes. No trees to dampen the sun or cast shadows. No flowers. This was a statement to space, and the ownership of it.

Beyond this was the house, a three-story affair painted brilliant white that wanted to cast a reflection in the grass if it was a perfect world. It was just as she remembered it. Not a degree larger or smaller. She had been here before, years ago. Her mother had dropped Hettie off at the Valancourt house for Avery's tenth birthday. She wasn't invited, of course. Only two girls from her class received an invitation. The rest of the invites went to junior high kids, even a few high schoolers. It was rumored the Mayor made an appearance, but that was never verified, and Hettie couldn't know for sure, as she never went inside. After walking toward the house just long enough for her mother to pull their Volvo away from the curb and back to their own modest side of town, she sat down in the middle of that endless expanse of green. Her poofy party dress, bought especially for the occasion and never worn afterward, had wrinkled, but never stained. Even the Valancourt grass withheld itself from Hettie. She sat there for three hours, hoping against instinct to make some sort of minor scene by her act of defiant longing, to be ushered inside by one of the partygoers that walked by her without looking in her direction, feet crunching on the combed white gravel of the driveway. But no one did, just like always. As the sun went down, she got up, walking home on stiff legs, and told her parents she got food poisoning, and was driven home by a very concerned Mrs. Valancourt, a plastic bucket held between her legs. Her mother's diatribe on the secret corporate ownership of the FDA and their cabal with Big Pharma to make people sick and keep them sick allowed

Hettie to escape to her bedroom where she waited for tears that never came, leaving her awake and dreaming with eyes wide open about how things should have been instead of how they really are.

Seven years later, now it was Hettie that walked up the driveway, her own shoes crunching on that same white gravel. Her graduation was finally complete, and she made a pact with herself that if she knocked on the door, attempted to enter under normal terms and conditions, then she certainly couldn't be blamed for how she actually ended up inside the home. She made many pacts with herself like this. It's how she got all of those phones, and so much more that no one knew about. Her secret negotiations.

Mounting the wraparound porch, framed by six stately columns of what looked like marble but was probably something far more exotic, she skipped the doorbell and rapped on the thick wood of the double door. It echoed on the other side, as if bouncing off totally empty drywall and hardwoods polished by hired hands, following the blue blood adage that coziness is the providence of the lower classes.

She didn't knock a second time. After a full two minutes, she stepped down off the porch and headed for the back yard. She hoped the Valancourts didn't have a dog, but knew that no animals would be allowed on the property, or would voluntarily choose to live there.

Her assumption proved correct. The back yard—the *grounds*, as it was probably referred to around a long dining room table—was almost a mirror image of the front. It stretched hundreds of yards back to a bone white privacy wall that rose twenty feet high. No vines or shrubbery or fountains of naked children that would add a blue blood touch of 'big R' Romance.

Hettie looked up at the windows of the house, trying to suss out which room belonged to Avery, and if it had changed since she was a little girl. Pale curtains covered each, hiding the inside from outside envy, framed by black shutters like sideways eyelashes varnished with drag queen mascara. French doors led out to the brick patio on which Hettie stood. Out of curiosity, she tried the handle on the double French doors, giving her fingers something to do while she planned her ascent of a house exterior with no visible hand holds. It was unlocked. The back door to the most expensive house in town was open to the world. Hettie walked in. She needed no invitation this time.

What confronted her was a magazine shoot from *Architectural Digest*, lacking only camera and crew. Stiff Scandinavian furniture that invited no one to sit. Tan leather-bound books no one read. Modernist works of art and bland imported curios that no one understood. White, grey, and black. A celluloid negative passed off as a photograph. This was a place where no one lived. They passed through the rooms, on their way to somewhere else. But no living took place here. No memories were created, no shared moments. It was a set. Stage dressing for a scripted play performed by tired actors with the next gig on their mind. Hettie's heart tightened, not with sadness, but with longing. It was everything she wanted.

She climbed the wide stairs to the second floor, and tried each closed door, finding empty rooms behind each, until she found what must have been the place where Avery slept. It was painted a pale pink and grey in a chevron pattern. A chandelier hung where most rooms suffered a wood panel ceiling fan. There was a dresser with perfume bottles and a lotion set, a desk holding up a single jewelry box, and a bed. Queen size. Every pillow had a store display stiffness to it. Not one makeup stain on the sheets, pulled back in a stiff ribbon. The wall next to the window featured the sort of standard fare teenage girl collage that was born in a production designer's fading memory, built from fashion magazine advertisements and clickbait *Cosmo* articles, all professionally rendered, framed, and mounted. A photograph-quality painted portrait of Avery was hung on the wall opposite her bed. It captured her beauty, the shine of her black hair, the upturn at the edge of each eye, the symmetry of her features, but somehow lacked the sadness and mystery that was always just under Avery's well-rehearsed smile. There was magnetism, but no nuance. No enigma. The painting looked two-dimensional. One-dimensional, if that was even possible. The artist obviously didn't know her at all, not like Hettie did.

Turning her back on this monstrosity, Hettie opened the closet door and stepped inside. It was bigger than her own bedroom, more of a live-in than a walk-in, and featured a Broadway vanity, mirrored wall, shelving, and rows of clothes, hung according to color and season, anchored below by hundreds of ridiculously expensive shoes arranged on display racks. The air smelled lightly of expensive perfume and that plastic scent of all high-end retail stores stuffed with unworn fabric.

She pulled off her left shoe—a canvas slip-on that she always wore—and sock, and slipped her bare foot into one of the shoes, a gold, serpentine number with reptilian brocade and a six-inch spiked heel. Her feet weren't necessarily larger than Avery's, but they were a different shape, wide where she was narrow, so the bends of the shoe bit into her skin in strange places. It felt wonderful. Hettie stuck out her foot toward the mirror, admiring how her leg ended in such a beautiful arrangement of leather and straps, and the perfectly unscuffed red sole reflecting back at her. She smiled.

Moments later, she was wearing one strappy heel and one knee-high boot, and trying on anything that looked like it wouldn't fit her. Jeans, gowns, hoodies, scarves made from an entire barnyard full of different animals dyed a rainbow of unnatural colors. Going for the cocktail dresses, Hettie pulled aside a swath of looked-over clothes and found writing on the closet wall. "FUCK ME" was scrawled in lipstick. A statement? A *command?* She bent her toes inside the boot and sighed with the pain.

Back out in the bedroom proper and back in her own clothes, Hettie lay on the bed, leaving room for another person next to her. She rolled onto her side, away from the portrait. She imagined lying here with Avery, the real Avery with all of her dimensions, talking about all those clothes, telling each other secrets. Hettie would offer advice on any number of topics that had nothing to do with boys, pulling from her vast knowledge of *Redbook* and *Good Housekeeping* that she read from cover to cover at the many doctor's office visits she endured as a child. Avery would marvel at Hettie's wisdom. Then she'd cry, the reality of her hopeless situation again breaking back in on her, and Hettie would hold her and all would be right in the world. She'd be her protector. She'd be her everything. What else would they need? Exactly nothing, that's what.

A tear rolled down Hettie's cheek. Such a monumental waste. All of it.

She raised her arms above her head and slid her hands under the pillow. Her fingers grazed something furry, and she pulled a stuffed animal from where it was hidden like a lost tooth, waiting for a midnight fairy. It was scruffy, its features rubbed away, the only thing in the room that had any wear on it. It must have been a cat, or a bunny. Probably a bunny. Hettie looked into its blank face and asked the bunny its name. It told her.

X.

Later that night, Hettie lay on her own bed, squeezing the stuffed animal in her left hand. She was on her back, her legs bent underneath her, like she slid to a stop. Her body always got itself into this shape when she was lost in thought and didn't know what her limbs were doing. It was just easier for her to think this way. She sent out her mind to the hospital, to find Avery and tell her it was going to be okay. She closed her eyes and repeated the words she had bought that would allow her the ability of astral projection. Her bunny was safe, and Hettie would bring it to her, she just had to tell her how. She held up the small toy and waited, whispering her words, then sat quietly, listening.

Something deep inside her ears vibrated, every hair on her arms and legs standing up straight. It hummed, then spread out into a melody. Music, coming from elsewhere in the house. It sounded ambient, like a film score. "Fuck me," Hettie grumbled as she threw aside the stuffed animal and jumped out of bed.

Downstairs smelled like popcorn. It was the second Tuesday of the month, which—according to the rustic chalkboard in the kitchen—meant "Bad Movie Night." The television flickered in the den, backed by the electronic spike of '80s synth music. Her parents had rented a C-grade train wreck from the last store in town that not only offered rentals, but rented them in VHS. They were purists, down to the thematic elements, only renting movies made before the post-irony '90s which were so inscrutably earnest and lacking in any sort of self-awareness or concept of parody that Hettie could barely understand what was happening on-screen. Like it was a sketch comedy send-up of a real motion picture.

Tonight it was her mom's turn to pick the bad movie, and she chose *The Last Boys*, a shoestring knock-off of the classic California vampire flick that should have looked and sounded like a music video, back when they still made music videos, but instead looked like a home movie shot with one of those enormous video cameras large enough to accept an actual VHS, recording straight to magnetic tape. This was a bootleg homage to one of the films her parents saw together in college when they were 'courting,' as her dad phrased it, which always made Hettie imagine a royal throne room crowded with costumed attendants, all watching her parents eat dinner together at some cheesy neon diner, holding hands across the Formica table, admiring the other's gelled hair and neon clothing.

Hettie stood in the doorway to the den, behind the couch where her parents were draped over each other like overheated teenagers. Her father had his hand on her mother's left breast. She didn't want to know where his other hand was.

On the screen, beach punk vampires were eating Chinese food in their boho underground lair that looked more like someone's basement than an actual boho underground lair. The vamps were clowning Mitchell, the initiate, with various food-related illusion pranks, stoner laughs, and bland mockery an octave too low, inserted during post-production through bad ADR. It was a very stagey scene, even amid an incredibly stagey movie.

The blonde mullet vampire, obviously the leader because his makeup was better, made Mitchell eat maggots. He didn't appreciate that very much, and told him so, before dropping his takeout box, exposing the maggots to be merely white rice. There seemed to be fuzz and other gunk scattered throughout the rice, as if they had to retake that scene a few times, and only had room in the budget for one box of rice. The other vampires found this hilarious. Supernatural creatures must set the humor bar lower than those burdened with mortality.

The blonde mullet vampire apologized in an exaggerated take on sarcasm that made it seem like it was dubbed into English by a non-English speaker. "No hard feelins, huh?" he said, clapping Mitchell on the back.

With a whisper into the ear of another vampire that had a dirty blonde afro that somehow ended in a mullet, a bottle was produced, covered in a metallic casing most likely inspired by a cursory browse at Pier One Imports. The blonde mullet vampire took a drink, then offered it to Mitchell, who seemed dubious. That, or the cheap Chinese food wasn't agreeing with him.

Blonde mullet vampire shook the bottle, exhorting Mitchell to join them. *Become* one of them. A brotherhood of bad hair and eternal life. All he had to do was take a drink.

Either not believing that the wine was blood, or befuddled from a bout of intestinal duress, Mitchell received the Pier One bottle and took a drink, eschewing the warning of the '80s boho version of the Manic Pixie Dream

Girl, who was skulking in the background the entire time. This stuff in the bottle was obviously wine. Not blood. Not poison blood. Oh, Mitchell, you fucking dummy!

Mitchell drank deeply, finishing every last drop of the liquid in the bottle.

Blonde mullet vampire laughed ruefully, apparently trained at the old timey villain school of villainous laughter. Then he clapped that slow clap, taken up by the rest of his crew. He stood, clapped Mitchell on the back and called him "bro," informing him that he'd never, *ever* grow old, and he'd never, *ever* die, but he would have to eat, and he clearly wasn't talking about Chinese food.

"Well," said one of the other dude vampires who looked like a girl with incredibly teased hair and an exposed midsection. "Not all the time."

All the glam rock vampires laughed, joined by Hettie's parents, who threw popcorn at the screen, commenting about how the script wasn't even close to *The Lost Boys*, which somehow made the movie so much better. Hettie might have laughed with them, from her hiding spot, but by then she wasn't listening.

Somehow, in some bizarre way, the cheesefest she just witnessed struck her profoundly, the line echoing and repeating back to her, becoming less corny with each repetition. The inner gong sounded inside her brain, for the second time in the same week.

You'll never, ever *grow old, bro. You'll never,* ever *die.*

She again lay on her bed, staring at the ceiling, her eyes blinking quickly, the bunny once again in her hands. The words had worked.

You'll never, ever *die.*

Finally, she startled herself by jumping from her bed and pulling the iPhone from under it. She typed in a few words, waited for faraway servers to pull up the knowledge, then read.

XI.

Twelve hours and two buses later, set into motion by a vague excuse about "extracurricular research at the library" to her parents, Hettie walked up to a run-down storefront in the dingier part of town near the community college. The neighborhood was rapidly gentrifying, but still cheap and sullied enough to host offbeat stores such as this one. Hettie looked down at the piece of paper in her hand, where the words "Sanctum Magickal Bazaar" were written. They matched the sign, almost down to the exact Gothic font.

Wind chimes tinkled as the door opened, accented by the actual sound of wind, that must have come from an electronic device. Good. Anyone who took their front door first impression this seriously must have the answers she was looking for. The shop was small and claustrophobic in layout, which wasn't helped by the floor to ceiling racks stuffed with crystals and amulets and books and every sort of arcana a community college student would ever need. The place smelled of a heavy, sickly sweet incense and oily candles. It was cloying, not like the smell of Pier One, where the blonde mullet vampire picked up his faux wine bottle. This incense had sweat in it. Jars of herbs lined the wall behind the counter, where a clerk stood reading from a scroll. An actual scroll. He was pale and balding, and wore a loose fitting purple shirt, with a string of puka shells wrestling with his sparse but very long and very black chest hair. Puka shells didn't seem very new agey. It seemed more frat boy douchey. He also wasn't wearing any shoes. The hair was just as long and black on his feet.

Hettie walked up and stood in front of the counter. Her heart thudded. Not because she was nervous or anything, this place scared her. Her pulse raced because she was in a hurry. If Avery died, there would be nothing Hettie could do. So, she cleared her throat. Twice.

After a moment, he nodded, then rolled up the scrolls with care and quite a bit of ceremony. He tied it firm with a piece of golden cord, then slid it into the sleeve of his shirt, before crossing his arms and regarding her with a sigh. "Can I help you?" he said, closing his eyes and keeping them closed for several seconds, during which time Hettie placed the stressor of the sentence on each word individually, still coming up with the same sense of put-upon annoyance. Framing your opening question as unbreakable sarcasm isn't an easy thing to pull off.

"I'm looking for books on vampires."

"Of course you are," he deadpanned, not even trying to hide his irritation.

"Not,"—she waggled her fingers around her face—"*those* kinds of vampires."

"Then what kind of vampires, exactly?"

"The real kind."

"The real kind," he repeated. This guy hadn't blinked since he opened his eyes again.

"I need to learn how to summon vampires. Or a vampire. I'll only need one."

"Maybe you can just leave out a bowl of blood on your back step, and they'll come flocking like feral cats."

"I know you think this sounds silly, or you're trying to make it incredibly clear that this sounds silly, but I also know that this is just a front. A dupe."

"A dupe." Deadpan alley had an echo.

"Yes, a dupe. The website I found—"

"Oh, you read a *website!*"

"—said that whomever worked here—"

"I *own* here, darling."

"—would act like they didn't know what you were talking about, but that they really do. That they—*you*—have a book, that isn't available online, that can summon vampires. I need that book, or just access to it. I can pay." Hettie opened her satchel and placed several large stacks of cash, wrinkled bills of various denominations wrapped in rubber bands, onto the glass countertop.

The man's eyes bulged, then narrowed. "Where does a girl your age get this kind of money?"

"I'm not at liberty to say."

The man looked at her, then threw his head back and unleashed a Broadway laugh that you could hear up in the penny seats. He clapped his hands, and kept the laugh going longer than was necessary.

"You're an odd duck, aren't you?"

"I guess I am." Hettie felt a sideways grin stretch her cheek. She liked the sound of that. Maybe she'd put it on her license plate someday when she decided it was time to start hating the planet and buy a car. ODDVCK.

The shop owner's whole demeanor changed, either due to her odd duck status, or the thousands of dollars she was carrying with very little regard for security. Probably the latter. Odd ducks were a dime a dozen. Rich ducks required many, many more dimes. "Follow me," he said.

He led her deeper into the store, which was only a few feet. "Regardless of what you read, we don't normally deal in the darker end of the spiritual spectrum, but we kept getting people like you coming through here that I figured we better start stocking some vampire stuff." He stopped at a very low, two-tiered wooden shelf. The top had a cat bed on it, and in front of it was a litter box. Paperbacks held sway in the middle. "We keep them back here so the teeny boppers have to walk through the entire store to look for their Team Edward or Team Whateverthefuck fan club stuff."

"I've never seen those movies."

"Yeah, and I've never seen *The Fast and the Furious.*"

Hettie looked through the books, which were mostly all fan fiction and cheap rip-offs of mainstream novels, with lots of long hair and open shirts. There were a few self-published history books on vampires and vampirism, something that looked like a wacky vampire comedy, along with some locally sourced supernatural erotica. Each cover was worse than the last. "Are these all of your books on the topic?"

"Yes. We're an esoterica shop. Not a horror store."

"But the website said—"

"You sure they spelled it right? There's another store that spells 'Magick' without the 'K' that's up in Portsmouth. They're way more into the hardcore occult stuff. Black magic and conjuring and all of that. We get our signals crossed sometimes. Works out for both of us, most of the time."

Hettie pulled the paper from her pocket. Sure enough, no "K." Just regular old Magic. She folded the paper and put it back into her pocket.

"You give me a hundred bucks, you can have the whole lot."

"No thanks. None of these are what I need."

"Poke around online. You'll be shocked at what you'll find."

"I did. Lots of conflicting theories, message boards full of shit talking, some rituals, but ... I need something close. Something in town. I need ..." She didn't know how to put it into words, especially because it didn't make any sense to the person she was before Avery got sick.

The shop owner thought for a second, then raised his finger as an idea came to him, like they do in the movies. "I saw a post about Nightvayne Ravenscroft doing a reading at one of those bullshit bookstores out in the boonies."

The obscene alteration gave her pause, but only for a second. "Who?"

"Who what?"

"Who's this Ravenscraft whatever?"

He leveled her a 'you've got to be fucking kidding me look.' Her blank stare moved him to put it into words. "You've got to be fucking kidding me."

She shrugged.

"You don't get out much, do you?"

"Not if I can help it."

"Nightvayne Ravenscroft only sold about fifty billion books last year, all of them about vampires. She claims that she knows a few of them personally through some hook up in the supernatural underground. They tell her stories, and she adapts them into her novels. Her Dark Muses, she calls them. I guess it makes for some popular books. No real gore, but lots of romance and missionary sex. Lots of adjectives, too. Real lace curtain kind of stuff. Not that I ever read any of them …"

Hettie was about to say something, but the man cut her off.

"Okay, maybe one, or probably two. Yeah, definitely three, but that's only because I was seeing this guy who wouldn't stop talking about them and left them at my house and … What was his name? Okay, I read four of her books, but only liked one of them."

She waited to make sure he was done. He was. "Which one?"

"Which book? I can't remember the—"

"No, I mean—"

"*The Bleeding Moon.* Man, that ending …"

"No, which bookstore is the reading?"

The man seemed irritated that she had cut off his weak denial that no one asked for. "I don't know. You think I ever visit the suburbs?"

Hettie looked around. "We're *in* the suburbs."

"We're in *midtown*. I'm talking about the real suburbs. Strip malls. Fake Australian steak houses. Megachurches." He shivered, only half dramatically.

"But—"

"Do you want to argue about geographic labels, or do you want information on how to find a real-life vampire?"

"You think they'll have them there?"

He wrote down the name of the bookstore, and sketched out some quick directions and landmarks. "If there's a real vampire within five hundred miles of here, they'll be at that reading, either behind the microphone, or sitting in the audience, soaking in all that dolled up prose." He handed her the paper.

"Is *she* a vampire?"

"I guess there's only one way to find out."

She took the address gratefully. "Thank you."

"You're welcome." It was the most earnest he had sounded all day. Probably even longer than that.

Hettie smiled at him, then turned and headed toward the front of the store and the door.

"Hey you," the shop owner said.

She turned.

"You look too smart to think any of this is real."

Hettie glanced around the shop, at the crystals and sage and tapestries and chimes. She looked back at the man standing beside the cat bed. "So do you."

XII.

He wasn't kidding about the suburbs.

Hettie had no idea street numbers went up that high and still were considered part of a city. 245th Street? The bus kept forging ahead. They were going to hit the three hundreds soon. It seemed akin to dimensional travel. And yet the streets kept going, and so did the stores, and gas stations, boxy churches, fast food joints, and massive supermarkets, and the huge, angular, similar-looking houses that were grouped into spacious developments built over the graveyards of farmland, sporting names like Fox Run and Battle Creek. All attempting an East Coast vibe in title, but landing nowhere near the ocean. Towering model homes made to look like nineteenth century chalets that couldn't have been over five years old. Spindly trees no taller than a man were planted in each front yard, yoked by collars attached to metal poles. Maybe they needed to be shown how to grow up straight.

The bus was sparsely populated but an interesting mix. Small brown women from Guatemala or El Salvador or wherever else that wasn't Mexico sat cloistered together in their maid uniforms near the front, talking quickly in Spanish. Weekend office workers and carbon footprint warriors sat toward the middle, each leaned over their phones, all plugged into their headphones. In the back were obviously a few late arrivals to the Ravenscroft reading, underage goth girls who lacked driver's licenses but not money for expensive costumes. Corsets covered by felt soldier jackets and capes, fishnet stockings, complicated boots with impractical heels. Hair was either dyed black or hidden by imported wigs of real Indian tresses. Ankh necklaces and lots and lots of rings. Their makeup was dramatic and precise, whites, reds, and blacks, but made them look cheaper than they'd ever allow. No matter how hard they tried, they just couldn't pull it off and make it seem natural.

Hettie found herself staring at them, wondering what they'd fetch on the white slavery market. Probably not much. Too high maintenance. One of them, carefully skinny and tragically pale, bared her teeth and hissed at Hettie, looking for a reaction and getting very little in return. Her canines were long and filed to points. They could have been part of the costume, too, but it wasn't likely. Dentists would apparently do anything for a buck, including defacing a seventh grader and severely narrowing her future marriage and employment options. Could her parents know? How could they not?

Thoroughly unimpressed, Hettie turned back to the window, and imagined what her own parents would do if she came home with permanent fangs. They'd most likely discuss the merits of self-expression, and tie it to some ancient religious rite, finding value in some shitty act of teenage rebellion. Insurrection was only worthwhile when it caused a reaction. That was why Hettie was so morbidly square.

The streets went on and on, wide and in perfect order. This was unhurried real estate, gridded out generously for maximum monetizing while still giving the illusion of a semi-rural lemonade lifestyle. A family lived in each one of these homes, wobbling in their own personal orbit. Hettie had no idea this many people lived in her city. Where did they come from, and what were they doing out here, in this loosely attached smear of something that didn't look anything like her zip code? Maybe it wasn't. Maybe the zip code changed without fanfare and allowed this seepage away from the heart to spread out and fade into something else.

This journey to the hinterlands seemed to be taking her further away from her goal. Her head hurt, and she felt her blood pulsing behind her eyes. She hadn't been sleeping well. Too many dreams, and journeys outside herself alone in her room. And the research, sifting through the fangasm bullshit and genre insider backbiting for what might be real and true. It was getting exhausting. She squeezed the bunny inside her jacket. Hettie couldn't imagine finding what she so desperately needed way out here, in the middle of a gated nowhere. It was then that the bus braked and she saw the crowd gathered in the Gateway Plaza Supercenter parking lot. For a second she thought she was back in front of the hospital, but then quickly remembered that Avery was yesterday's news, and vampires were forever, which is exactly why she was here.

XIII.

The parking lot was a zoo, and even had a few animals. Well, reptiles and insects, perched on shoulders or crawling up bare arms, which still qualified, if one wanted to get technical.

The shop owner at the Magickal Bazaar was right for a second time—every spook and superfan from five hundred miles around was either inside the huge, chunky Barnes & Noble building, or trying to get in, playing monsters in the parking lot. The crowd had the look and feel of a Marilyn Manson concert combined with a steampunk convention running headlong into a boy band concert stop. Men and women, young and old, all shapes and sizes, sexual persuasions, and serotonin levels, had dressed up in their costumed best and come out for the urban fantasy event of the year. It wasn't every day that a bestselling author made an official visit to this town, especially a megawriter so dedicated to her fans, who loved her for it. Hettie learned on the bus ride over that Ravenscroft's social media pages were flooded with followers and always abuzz with activity, as she would personally post and interact with her readership several times per day, regardless of her schedule or deadlines. Critics who dared give less than glowing reviews were savaged online by dedicated internet honor warriors that made life so difficult for them that most genre bloggers and other professional reviewers stopped commenting on her books altogether, which somehow only seemed to increase sales. Victory was declared with each character assassination and electronic takedown, further building camaraderie amongst the 'Ravens,' insulating millions of disaffected or misunderstood readers against the harsh rebuke of the outside world and creating a pleasant, perfectly controlled echo chamber inside Ravenscroft fandom. It was the ideal terrarium for those who either feared or disliked (the former usually leading to the latter) mainstream society, although that line was blurring by the day, as a scene from the fringes was slowly absorbed by the middle. And it made the author something very close to a religious figure, and even closer to a billionaire. Oprah housewives didn't have anything on an unkindness of Ravens.

Hettie understood all of this, as she knew that she hadn't nor would she probably ever fit into the workaday world. She just didn't like vampires.

But she didn't have to. She was here on a hunting mission. Hunters didn't have to like their prey or even respect it, as long as they could kill it and put it in a bag.

Amid the passing of parasols hiding pale skin from the setting sun, Hettie felt like all eyes—reshaped by surgery and makeup and most hidden by contacts of various levels of dramatic discoloration—were on her, but soon noticed that everyone was looking at everyone else, to find acquaintances and friends, to check out the latest in DIY vampire fashion, and probably more than anything to hook up. A gathering of the disaffected creates a feeding frenzy for so many things.

"Raven Stacy!" one of them said, reaching out long, black nailed hands.

"Raven Brinna!" answered the other as they touched palms and leaned in for two air kisses, European style. Their complicated hats and birdcage veils wouldn't let them within a foot of each other's faces.

Raven Simone, Raven Simone, Raven Simone kept looping inside Hettie's brain, and she shook off this personal aside, feeling an odd sense of being on safari in the hinterlands of her own city, before a sense of urgency snapped her back to her purpose. She needed to get inside and close to the author. If she wasn't totally full of shit, which was entirely possible, Ravenscroft could point Hettie in the right direction, or maybe even lead her there personally. She had to. Time was running out, and guides were hard to come by in this part of the world.

Hettie moved up and down the line. None of these saps or their fancy pets were getting inside. Ponytailed Barnes & Noble staff members paced the perimeter, obviously terrified about the number of people already in the store, muttering into headsets about maximum capacity and serious fire code violations. Hettie would have to find another way in.

She moved back from the crowd, to get a better feel for the layout, and spied the hissing girl and her friends clattering toward the back of the building. She followed, passing between the brown cement of the wall and the massive tour bus decorated with an enormous decal of a woman dressed in a Victorian gown, topcoat, and hat, lace spilling out of every opening of her outfit like a scarecrow leaking straw. This was Nightvayne Ravenscroft, right down to the stupid spelling, and she had her own Star Coach.

Rounding the corner, Hettie saw the emergency exit door slowly closing, directly adjacent to the loading dock. She surged forward and stuck her foot in the space between the door and the frame, then squeezed through. A store employee with a perfectly round goatee was looking down at the phone number written hastily in lipstick on his palm, transferring it to his phone as the excited giggles from the bus goths faded further into the stockroom, stacked floor to ceiling with books.

Hettie moved past him, but he held out his free hand. "No entry," he said, cleared his throat and slid his phone into his pocket as he got back into character.

She waved her school ID card at him and walked quickly past. "Press. Reporter from the Tribune."

"Oh, okay, but—"

"Sorry, I'm late. I'll fax you my credentials." She realized just how ridiculous that sounded, but it seemed to confuse him for just long enough before the back door opened again. Two middle-aged men who had no business wearing leather pants received the full frustrated brunt of the newly focused, last-minute security guard.

Hettie passed through well-lit shelves of crisp, unopened books. The air smelled of glossed ink and freshly cut paper. At the far end, a converted break room was blocked off with a velvet rope, colored blood red. They must carry this cliché from town to town on the bus. The door was ajar, and the sumptuous backstage area was empty of human beings, left stuffed with cushy couches, thick rugs, and black lace draping every light. Two security guards—women in identical suits and sunglasses, both with hair pulled into buns so flawless and tight they looked painful—flanked either side of the rope. By expression, posture, and something less tangible but abundantly obvious to the wary predator in all of us, these girls were total ass kickers. Hettie would never be able to get past them. The one on the left put finger to ear, checking in with the security detail in front. She nodded, and the other guard left her post and passed through the door separating the front and the back of the store, checking the holster under her sharp blazer as she went. This was some pre-scandal Secret Service level security. For an author, Ravenscroft must be very important, very wealthy, or piss off a lot of people. *Or perhaps all three*, Hettie thought, before cocking an eyebrow as an idea seized her. She disappeared back into the stock room, casting up a prayer to any god that would listen to grant her an abandoned scrunchie.

She reemerged moments later, hair gathered into a frizzy ponytail poorly held by a rubber band and affected the rushed pace of a Barnes & Noble employee, marching past the remaining security guard, opening the access door that led into the store proper and emerging into a darkened and hushed sales floor, hazy with smoke and mood music. Moving past row after deserted row of neatly arranged books, she arrived at the back ring of five hundred super fans of Nightvayne Ravenscroft, pressed together as tightly as they could without mushing each other's costumes. The air smelled of sweaty anticipation, and a touch of body odor, masked by patchouli, incense, and expensive French perfume, heavy on the ambergris.

In the middle of all of this made-up humanity sat the author on a raised dais, perched on the edge of a plush Victorian wing back armchair, hair that was too silvery white to be anything other than an expensive dye job catching the spotlight and illuminating her like a savior dressed in black velvet. She turned a page in her book and continued reading, backing music swelling at rehearsed spots to heighten the tension of the prose.

"*She knew, on that night of nights,* [music sting] *with the moon shining above their naked bodies like a bloated egg,* [music swell] *that she would join the legion of the damned.* [distant thunder crash] *She would become mistress of snake and worm and all dark places. She would become a feaster of blood, she would become vampire incarnate.*" [scream]

The entire crowd gasped, whispered invocations, and raised arms in supplication, thumbs hooked together, flapping their hands like they were making a shadow puppet of a bird, or a bat. Fingertips touched together in a strangely quiet form of applause that sounded more like the mass rustling of broken wings than clapping.

The author continued with a new chapter, so Hettie had time, but she needed to get into position before it was over, to state her case. She pulled a hardcover book from the nearby celebrity non-fiction shelf and set it on the ground, spine down, pages fanned out like a peacock's tail. She took a lighter from her pocket and lit one end of the pages, then retreated through the door into the storeroom. The flames were ignored at first, as they seemed part of the showy atmospherics of the reading while all eyes were on the stage. Hettie threw another book onto the other, then another. In seconds, it became a serious bonfire. Nearby fans squawked, as did security radios. The crowd scattered, the music died, and the lights came up. Ravenscroft was whisked from the stage by three female security guards, all nearly identical to the two backstage, guns trained on the crowd. A few people screamed.

A few more cried. Someone yelled that it was Paris all over again. Another shouted Ray Bradbury's name. Store employees tried to stop people from leaving with unpurchased books in their hands, but they were pushed aside or trampled as everyone made for the front exit. The reading was over.

Backstage, the converted break room/now green room swathed in black and red velvet was abuzz with activity. Legal experts, agents, and road managers were all on their phones with various agencies, calming nerves, changing plans, and filing claims. Either way, they'd all get paid.

Ravenscroft collapsed on one of the couches, leaning back to untie her tightly corseted midsection, exhaling with a moan when it finally came undone. "What the fuck happened out there?" She spoke to the room, which collectively paused, looking at each other, waiting for the first up to the line.

"Book fire," one of the security guards said, straightening up. This was obviously the captain of the quartet.

"Near the religious section," another added. "We think it was intentional."

Ravenscroft snorted, pulling off her wig and tossing it at one of her assistants, who caught it gingerly and carefully carried it to the crowded makeup counter. "Fucking Bible bangers." She ran her hands along her closely cropped blond hair, scratching her scalp.

"Has to be," an assistant said.

"Westboro, probably," offered another. Both of the assistants set about removing Ravenscroft's complicated costume.

"Sending another message," the captain said.

"Those motherfuckers," Ravenscroft sneered, lighting a cigarette.

"We couldn't find any protestors out front."

She exhaled a plume of smoke. "They must be going low-key. Getting inside."

"Getting closer."

"We'll double security," said the other security guard.

"No, you'll do your fucking job next time or I ship your sorry asses back home. Maybe get some military types. SEALs or Rangers or whatever. Maybe get some men."

The faces of the female security guards showed no reaction. A vein bulged in the temple of the captain, who was about to say something when a stifled sneeze issued from behind a corner of drapery.

Ravenscroft scurried backwards on the couch. "Who's that?"

"Come out from behind the drapes!" the captain yelled, drawing her sidearm.

The fabric bunched, then billowed. Guns were pointed and hammers cocked as Hettie stepped from one of the heavy drapes. She got caught in the folds, and it took her longer than was gracious to get free. "I didn't mean to sneak," she said quietly, rubbing lint from under her nose.

"Don't you *fucking* move!" the captain shouted, sounding like something a security captain would say in a movie.

Hettie didn't.

"Identify yourself!"

"I'm Hettie."

"Are you Westboro?"

"Who?"

"Are. You. *Westboro?*"

"No."

"Who sent you?" Ravenscroft interjected, if only partially to stop the overdramatic captain show. "Pastor Skip?"

"*Pastor?*" Hettie laughed with such surprise that she snorted. "That's a good one. I'm agnostic."

"And I'm officially freaked," Ravenscroft said. "Get this weirdo out of here."

The guards moved toward her slowly, guns still raised. "I need to ask you something," Hettie said to Ravenscroft, "but I need to ask you alone."

Two security guards flanked Hettie and each grabbed an arm, while the assistant ran forward, wig in hand, nearly tripping in his panicked haste.

Ravenscroft waved him off. "How did you get in here?" she asked Hettie as she was pulled from the room.

"I just walked in."

"Someone—*everyone*—is getting fired for this!"

"I need to ask you if you'll help me. If you'd help my friend."

"Doug!"

A slick looking man in a shiny purple suit, presumably Doug, stepped from the entourage loosely circling the room. He pulled papers from a manila envelope and handed them to Hettie, holding a Waterman pen as thick as a carrot. "Non-disclosure agreement. Print name and sign." He didn't even look her in the face.

Hettie took the pen and fought to get her fingers around the bulky circumference, printing and signing as she was directed. Not because she was scared, but because she didn't care either way. She didn't have time to argue the ridiculousness of an author protecting her penchant for wigs.

Ravenscroft leaned forward in her chair, nearly pinching in half the cigarette between her fingers as she pointed at Hettie like a drill sergeant. "If you so much as *whisper* anything you saw back here today, you frumpy little twat, I'll sue you for everything you have, your parents have, everything your children will have, and their children after that. I'll make sure your bloodline is in court until the end of time."

Hettie finished signing and handed the pen back to Doug, who was already folding the papers back up and retreating deeper into the room, dabbed at his forehead.

"Now get the fuck out of here."

Exactly seven seconds later, Hettie was firmly ejected from the room by the two silent security guards, and the door slammed, muffling Ravenscroft's tirade at her staff. The lights went off above the door, and Hettie knew the whole circus was pulling up stakes and moving to the next town, never to return.

A surprised laugh came from behind her. "Holy shit, were you just hanging out with Ravenscrust?"

Hettie turned and found three people—two guys and a girl—standing at the entrance to the storeroom, all wearing understated but still very Victorian-influenced outfits. Hettie wasn't sure who asked the question, as they all sort of looked alike, and she imagined they all sounded similar. She nodded her head. They reacted together.

"I knew she was back there still," one of the guys said. "You said she was on the bus."

"Who cares," said the girl, rolling her eyes to what was probably the nape of her neck. "Why do you care?"

"What was she like?" the second guy asked Hettie. He was more handsome than the other, and smiled when he talked, exposing perfect teeth. Not a fang among them.

"Mean."

They all laughed.

"I told you," the first guy said. "I *told* you! She's an asshole. Everyone on the boards says she's an asshole."

"She cursed a lot," Hettie said. "Like, *a lot*."

"Of course she did. She's an asshole." The first guy wanted to make sure everyone knew he was right.

"She called me a twat."

The trio all put hands to mouths in surprise and joyous outrage.

"She wears a wig, too."

Now they fell into each other. "*Ooooooh!*"

"Redhead?" the girl asked.

"Blonde. Super short. Buzz cut, almost."

They all laughed again. The good looking guy slapped the other. "You owe me five bucks, dickhead."

"I knew it. I just *knew* it," the first guy said. "Total closet norm."

"What a fucking hack," the girl said.

Hettie was confused. "But ... then why are you all waiting back here, backstage, if you know that she's mean and think she's a hack?"

The second guy smiled. You could tell he was fully aware he looked more handsome when he smiled. "Because we knew you'd be here." Nothing but teeth.

"Really?"

"No, not really," the girl said. "Gods, don't be so gullible. He's just trying to get into your pants."

The thought of him getting inside of her pants or anything else that was hers made Hettie sick to her stomach.

"We came to clown the poseurs," the first guy, quickly becoming the other guy, said.

"You think these people are poseurs?"

"Of course. Did you see them?"

A spark of hope lit Hettie's eyes. "And you guys ... You guys are ... *real?*"

"Real as they come."

"So, you're vampires?" Hettie's voice went up an octave as it dropped to a whisper. Could this have just fallen into her lap? She dreamed something like this would happen, but she never knew when she could trust her dreams. They lied to her so many times. She was barely able to hear herself over her pounding heart.

The girl's heavily made-up eyes drooped into her cheeks and her mouth hung open with incredulity. "You can't be serious."

"I think she's serious," Mr. Dreamboat said.

"Maybe we *are* vampires," said the other guy.

"Don't be stupid," the girl said to him.

"No, we are. Why not?"

Hettie was crestfallen, and visibly slumped. How could she have believed that these three were anything other than bored. "Then ..." Hettie started. "Nevermind."

"What?" the girl asked. She seemed fascinated with Hettie, like she was looking at a different species that could speak perfect English.

"It's just that I need to find ... No. No, nothing. You'll think it's stupid. It is stupid. The whole thing ... I'm going home." Hettie started for the back exit, retracing her steps in what had turned out to be a colossal waste of time, when she—when *Avery*—could least afford it.

"I think she's looking for a vampire," Dreamy said.

"No ... You think?" The other guy was incredulous.

"You, wait," said the girl, jogging after Hettie.

Hettie didn't. The girl caught up, positioning herself in front of Hettie and cutting her off.

"You're literally, like, *actually* looking for a vampire?"

"Yes."

"Why?"

Hettie just stared at her. If she was another girl, or even another kind of girl, she would have probably started crying from the stress and the waiting and the frustration, but she wasn't, so she didn't.

"No answer?"

"It's extremely important," Hettie whispered. "It's ... a matter of life and death."

"Life and death, huh?"

Hettie nodded.

"Or maybe eternal life and the end of death?"

Hettie said nothing. Her mouth went dry.

The girl looked over Hettie's shoulder, at the two guys. "Should we tell her about the place?"

"No," the other guy said. "It's not for people like her."

Hettie turned around. "People like who?"

"Well, like you. You know ..." He put his hands up, as if he was going to act something out in the air, then dropped them and shrugged.

Hettie's eyes narrowed, lit up from within. "You don't know me. You don't know what I've done. What I'm willing to do."

Three smiles faded on three slightly made-up faces.

"Okay, let's tell her," Dreamboat said.

"It's your funeral," said the other guy, irritated at Hettie's slightly agro reaction to his last statement.

"No, but it might be hers."

"Please tell me." Hettie's voice sounded different. Not pleading, but soft, sad. Heartbroken. She didn't normally sound like this.

Dreamboat broke first. "It's called *Salon Éternelle*, heavy on the French accent. It's a … club, I guess. Guest list only. Exclusive, snooty. For the hard cores. The real deals. It's probably what you're looking for."

"Can you get me in?"

"No," said the other guy.

"Maybe," said the girl.

"*Probably*," said Dreamy. "No guarantees, but …"

"What?"

"You can't go dressed like that," said the girl, almost enjoying the statement. How many times had she heard that in her own life?

Hettie looked down at her outfit. "No?"

"No."

"So then, what do we do?"

"We go shopping."

XIV.

Three of them rode in the back seat of a custom BMW sedan, Hettie sandwiched on wood trimmed leather seats between the other guy and the girl. Dreamboat was driving, and kept repositioning the rearview mirror to get a better look at Hettie, who didn't notice, as she was watching her two seatmates pass a CD case striped with tiny lines of white powder chopped into even rows with a razorblade. The car hit a bump, and the girl nearly jammed the rolled bank note up her nose, smearing a few of the lines.

"Jeeves, watch your speed!" she said. "Mommy and daddy are ruining their futures back here." She finished, and passed it to the guy.

"Sure you don't want one?" he asked Hettie as the case moved past her.

She shook her head and mumbled something about allergies. The guy shrugged again—a specialty of his—and bent to his business. She'd just as soon swallow a bullet as shove industrial solvents up her nose. Did they have any idea what that was doing to their insides? Maybe they were vampires, and therefore immortal, so snorting crystal posed no danger to their long-term survival prospects. Hettie wondered how many layers of lies were built up to keep a vampire safe in a world where no one understood them and most wanted them dead.

"What's your name?"

Hettie snapped her attention back to the car, and the front seat, where Dreamboat was watching, waiting for her to answer his question, which she did. "Hettie."

The girl coughed, swallowing hard several times and rubbing the side of her nose. "Hettie? Is that your coven name?"

Hettie looked at her blankly.

"So, your *real* name is Hettie?"

"Yes."

"You don't hear that much around here," Dreamboat said. "Or anywhere, really. Not anymore."

"My parents named me after some beatnik named Hettie Jones."

"Lucky!" Dreamy said.

"The Beatniks are dead," the other guy mumbled, working his jaw.

"So are the Beatles," Dreamboat said, "and people still worship them."

"False idols."

"Hettie ... Hettie," the girl worked the name around her mouth, tasting it. "That's short for what? Heteeshia?"

"Hetero," chimed in the other guy.

"Henrietta," Hettie said.

"Oh," the girl said. "Henrietta isn't bad."

"Neither is Hettie." Dreamboat was probing hard, feelers fully extended. She could almost see his smile through his head from the back seat.

"Both are awful," Hettie said. "Don't you think?"

"These days?" said the girl. "People would kill for something old school stuffy like that."

"But Henrietta Wexler?" Hettie said. "Do you know hard it is to walk around with Henrietta Wexler hanging from your neck when everyone else is a Juniper or Clover or Emersyn or Lux? Or Avery ..." Her eyes unfocused.

"That girl on the news is named Avery," said Dreams.

"Rich cunt," muttered the girl.

"Such language!" The other guy said, then laughed.

Hettie's cheeks flushed with anger and she turned seething eyes to the girl, who was looking out the window, chewing the inside of her cheek. The CD case lay loosely on her lap, eyed by the other guy.

"HW," Dreamboat said. "Sounds important."

She blinked. "But no one ever called me HW. They called me Waxy Wexler. Henry Sexler. Wexy No Sexy."

"Who did this?" Dreamboat seemed genuinely concerned. This probably worked on absolutely everybody.

"Can you give me that, for fucksake?" The guy reached for the CD case. The girl handed it to him absently.

"Everyone from third grade on up," Hettie said. "Boys, mostly, but some girls, too."

"Children should be eaten before they can breed," the girl said. "All of them."

"Amen, sister," said the other guy, holding his breath after doing a line, his Adam's apple dancing inside his neck.

"Well, Henrietta Wexler," the girl said, sitting up straighter and rubbing her nose, "I'm Ruby. And this is Benthic." She pointed her chin toward the guy on the other side of Hettie. "And our pilot for today's flight is Ever."

"Hello."

"Those aren't our real names," Ever said.

"I know."

"But yours has *gotta* be Hettie," Ruby said.

Everyone agreed, even Hettie. They all rode in silence for a while, no one listening to the low ambient metal moaning from the speakers.

Benthic swirled his index finger across the last remnants of powder on the CD case, then rubbed. Smacking his lips, he leaned back and looked Hettie up and down like a judge on a television fashion design show. "So, about your ..." He made circular gestures with his hand. "Whole thing. What are we to do about this, Ruby?"

"There's a not-totally-horrendous costume shop at Oakview," Ever said.

"Bourgeois bullshit," Benthic sneered.

Ruby joined his expression. "Bootleg Party City."

"Party City *is* bootleg Party City," Benthic said.

"Could work in a pinch," Ever said.

"And this definitely is a pinch," Ruby said.

It all sounded like a scripted scene. These three had obviously spent a lot of time together, read the same blogs and deep web message boards, complained about the same issues over their unfiltered red wine, then waiting for some 'norm' to happen by so they could unleash another performance. Hettie was beginning to despise them, but knew that they were the best lead she had so far. She'd ride this train until it was clear it was taking her in the wrong direction, and then she'd hop off at the nearest station.

"You got money?" Benthic asked Hettie.

"Yes," she said.

"Good, you're paying our way in at the club. Finder's fee."

Ruby nodded. "Bennie makes a strong point. Consignment for the dark side."

"Rent." Ever stared at her again. His comment landed with a flat note this time, hard and tinny. No one said anything after that.

A few minutes later, the BMW pulled into the Oakview shopping center, which featured big box stores, anchored at each entry street by chain eateries lit up in neon. They had driven for what seemed like an hour, and the scenery hadn't changed one bit. An obese family walked out of the nearest restaurant, all wearing one of the free paper hats they give away at dinner.

The children were screaming and running amok. The parents both stared at their phones. This, naturally, started up the script between the three perfectly matched friends.

                              RUBY
              I want to kill every person in this world.

                             BENTHIC
         Patience, darling. Patience. Ammo doesn't grow on trees.

                              RUBY
                       But these monkeys do.

                              EVER
                           They're food.

                              RUBY
                Well, they certainly are what they eat.

                             BENTHIC
                        I'm losing my appetite.

                              RUBY
           Pull in over to the side. I'm gonna need to break out
           another baggie before I face what's waiting for us."

She knew that she was being dramatic, and it was mostly a figure of speech, but Hettie honestly wanted to kill herself at that very moment rather than spend one more second with this walking, talkingtalkingtalking and constantly sniffing sitcom. While they again cut up lines and passed around the CD case, Hettie closed her eyes, and checked in on Avery the best she could.

XV.

The foursome walked into the costume store, two of them high as fucking kites, the other two trying to feel each other out. This was a second-tier costume and hobby shop trying to hold on in a different marketplace populated by chain stores with much more vigorous buying power. It couldn't decide what exactly it wanted to be, so it offered cheap plastic masks and dusty props, higher priced costumes, and an assortment of wigs that must have appealed to a year-round clientele. Rows of white styrofoam heads painted with eyes and lips were topped with weirdly realistic wigs and hair pieces.

Ruby ran up and down the aisles, screaming a drawn out *"Booooo!"* at everyone she passed. For someone who claimed to despise everything, it was achingly apparent that she needed a massive amount of attention.

Hettie was in the women and girls' section, checking out tacky vampire costumes, as well as slutty versions of every fairly recognizable female character from fairy tale, animation, folklore, mythology, and motion pictures. Tarted up public figures of the past two centuries. Even more lascivious outfits were saved for professional vocations ranging from nurse to nun, with "Sexy" added to each. "Sexy Lumberjack." "Sexy Maid." "Sexy Cafeteria Worker." The costume industry was the last holdout amid the sexual revolution.

"Do you have a more ... generous size?" Hettie asked a passing employee, holding up a sheer, high collared black dress, most likely made in a Chinese sweatshop to closely match the outfit worn by Maleficent in the Disney movie. The tag was labeled with an "L" but based on its unusual cut and overall size, that letter clearly meant something else.

The clerk scratched at the patchy beard on his receding chin and hmmed to himself like he was pondering the secrets of the universe. After many moments, he puffed out his cheeks and rendered his answer from on high. "We have a vampire cape in a boys' husky."

Hettie's cheeks burned. Ruby slinked past the clerk. "This one will do." She pushed Hettie toward the changing room. "Get on in there, husky boy."

Inside the tiny, high-walled room, Ruby made a few last minute adjustments to the costume. Her hands shook, and her breath was quick and ragged. A weird grin was on her face, like she was trying to hold back an insane laugh.

"Why do you do that to yourself?" Hettie said.

"Do what?"

"You know."

Ruby was quiet for a moment, her hands moving even more quickly, tugging and tucking to make sure everything that was Hettie's fit inside the fabric. "It makes me feel like a different person."

Now Hettie was quiet. "Do you have any more?"

Ruby's smile was thin, and slightly sad. "Not for you." She stood back and put her hands on her hips. "Am I good, or what?" She stepped aside from in front of the mirror. "Take a look."

Hettie took in her reflection in the slightly distorted mirror. Her hands ran up and down the cheap, slick black fabric, tracing curves in her body that she herself rarely noticed, knowing full well that no one else around her had either. Her brow furrowed, and she pulled at lumps in the dress. "I look ridiculous."

"Says who?" asked Ruby.

"Says me."

"Says the fucking squares. The day people and the machine and the men that run it."

"Says me."

"You don't know what the fuck you're talking about."

"None of us do."

Ruby threw up her arms and started digging in her purse. "Jesus, Hettie …"

Hettie turned to the side, viewing herself in profile, appraising a different array of curves and lines. "I really have to wear this?"

"You do if you want to go," Ruby said, popping gum into her mouth and applying a new coat of blackish red lipstick in the mirror. "They have a dress code. Keeps out the norms, as it's a very focused sort of gathering. And you're definitely not a norm."

"No, she isn't a norm," Ever said, now standing in the doorway. "She's just dressed up as one."

"Yeah, she's a real freak," said Benthic, crouched in the corner. Hettie hadn't heard or seen either of them enter the changing area.

"Halloween all year long," Ruby added, finishing her lipstick and pouting her lips in the mirror.

Hettie could feel another semi-rehearsed back and forth building, so she gathered up her clothes and walked out of the dressing room. "Okay, time's a wastin'." She caught Ruby's smile as she went. "What?" Hettie asked.

The smile grew on Ruby's freshly darkened lips. "Nothing."

XVI.

Ever parked the BMW at the end of a cobblestone street, which was odd, as this city didn't have cobblestone streets. A Craftsman mansion far larger than the rest on the block, loomed at the end of a cul-de-sac lined by huge, centuries-old trees.

"That's got to be the place," Hettie said.

"She's a smart one, boys," Ruby said.

"Aren't they all," said Benthic.

Ruby and Benthic each did a line, then both cleaned the top of the CD case with respective index fingers before sticking them into their mouths and rubbing their gums.

"Let's go," Ruby said.

"Ha-lle-lu-jah!" Ever said with four pronounced syllables like a gospel preacher.

The foursome walked up the sidewalk. Ruby avoided the cracks and ridges caused by muscular roots from the Linden Oaks that had pushed up through the cement with a slow motion disdain for human pretense. Hettie detected motion in one of the cars parked along their route. It was a slightly rusted minivan, sun bleached to a neutral color made light blue in the sodium glow of the lone streetlamp. Inside sat a man in glasses, tie, and shirt sleeves, eating a sandwich while reading the paper, dabbing mayonnaise from his full moustache. The faintest sound of a ball game on the radio could be heard through the raised windows. The man didn't look up as they passed.

"This an all ages club?" Hettie asked, trying to remember the last time her own dad waited outside a shopping mall or concert while she filled her late childhood with late childhood activities.

The three looked at each other and giggled.

They reached the house, and Hettie made toward the steps leading up to the massive double doors marking the front entrance.

Ruby steered Hettie toward a side path heading to the back of the house, and down into a lightless stairwell. "It's down there."

Of course it is, Hettie thought. *Where else would it be?*

They descended the stairs in blindness. At the bottom, a small red light bulb offered a bit of murky, mood-setting illumination. Under the light stood a short, extremely muscular bouncer with a neck the same circumference as his head. He crossed his arms with difficulty and gave the group a suspicious once-over, leading to a twice- and a thrice-over.

Ruby nodded at the bouncer, who looked at Hettie. Not recognizing her, he pulled out a small black book and opened it, shining a pen light down onto the page. A small list of names written in tiny script filled a portion of the top sheet.

"Name," the bouncer said. His voice was extremely high. Almost comically so.

"Her name's not on it," Ruby said. "She's a pledge."

He closed the book and crossed his arms again with a creak of fabric or tendons or probably both.

"She's here for a reckoning."

The bouncer's exquisitely shaped left eyebrow raised halfway up his forehead. Her eyes now adjusted to the dim light, Hettie noticed that the man's features were all highlighted with flawless makeup.

"A rebirth."

The bouncer nodded, then motioned for Hettie to raise her arms. She did so and he waved a security wand up and down her body, front and back. Satisfied, he pressed the inside of her wrist with a metal stamp, the sort one would use to monogram a wax seal on a document. Hettie looked at her wrist, expecting a stylized black stamp, but found nothing. The bouncer motioned all of them to walk through the curtain behind him.

As Hettie passed, she noticed, then realized, that the man's whole face was drawn on in makeup. From the side, it was flat and featureless, like pale pumpkin pie painted with food coloring.

They walked the dark hallway, aiming toward the lighted room beyond. Sooner than expected, as if the last ten feet was suddenly erased, the foursome emerged into a candlelit cavern hollowed out of the foundation rock of the colossal mansion above it.

The floor was carpeted, and chairs were set up by the dozens in front of a low riser. Most of the chairs were occupied with the black forms of sitting people, some heads bowed, some faced the stage.

Toward the front row, a small flashlight waved and beckoned. Ruby dragged Hettie toward it, and the four took the last remaining seats in the front row. Girl girl, boy boy.

"Are you ready?" Ruby asked.

Hettie didn't answer. She wanted to shrug, but felt unable to do so.

A low positioned spotlight sparked and shined up into the face of a man, carving out his features in hideous lines of shadow.

"Are we all here?" the face asked.

"Some, not all!" answered the crowd so loudly that Hettie was startled.

"Are we all doomed?"

"We are!"

"Are you all looking for eternal life?"

"Yes," the crowd intoned in unison.

"Are you looking to wash away the now and stake your claim to a future that will not end?"

"Stake! Stake!"

"Do you seek paradise?"

"Yes!"

"Do you seek the blood? The blood that brings eternity?"

"Yes!"

"Will you accept the blood?"

"We will!"

Hettie's pulse quickened. She was on the verge of what seemed to be a mass inoculation. She reached for Ruby's hand, but couldn't find it. Instead, she clasped her palms together and thanked whatever dark gods ruled the forces outside of normal science. She prayed to the god of vampires, thanking her for this opportunity. It would not be in vain.

A tiny smile began to play on her lips at the unintentional pun in her prayer, when dual explosions of pyrotechnics went off on either side of the stage, and the house lights went on, flooding the room with harsh fluorescent bulbs set into office standard rectangles. Hettie nearly jumped out of her skin and looked at Ruby, who had her fingers in her ears, laughing wildly, as did everyone else in the room save for Hettie, who was pulled to her feet with the rest of the crowd as everyone started clapping. This wasn't a cavern. It was just a basement meeting room, with ceiling tiles, low carpeting, and paneled walls.

A very tan man with gelled up hair streaked with highlights, bounded back and forth across the stage, encouraging the crowd like a hip-hop hype man. He wore a Hawaiian shirt, cargo shorts, and unlaced high tops. Bad tribal tattoos could be seen on his chest and upper arms, pushing through the self-tanning spray. His arms and legs, and probably the rest of his body, seemed to be shaved and oiled up to shine in all their carrot-colored glory. This was the face on the stage, now looking nothing like it did out and away from the shadows.

"Good evening, children of the night, now children of the *Light*!"

"Good evening, Pastor Skip!" the crowd screamed back at him.

Pastor Skip leapt to the edge of the stage and shoved his microphone in the face of a gutter punk with more piercings than skin. "How are we doing on this fine night?"

"Blessed to be here, Pastor Skip!" The clanging of the metal in his lips clinked with every bilabial sound he made. Everyone applauded like a bipartisan state of the union address.

"You hear that, children? Blessed to be here. *Blessed* to be here. *Ahhh*-men?"

"*Ahhh*-men."

Hettie began to panic. This wasn't what she expected, wasn't what she was looking for. This was ... This was—

"When looking for the dark, don't forget the words of Mark: He that believeth and is baptized shall be saved; but he that believeth not shall be damned."

The crowd hooted and hollered. Mini mosh pits broke out, peppered with squeals and a "Heck yeah!" or two.

This ... Pastor Skip was ... *preaching*. Hettie's heart thudded inside her chest, and she was getting dizzy. It was the first legitimate fear she had felt in weeks, maybe months. Ever since the day the ambulance left the parking lot at school.

"Who needs books of sin when we have the book of living again?"

Good fucking Christ on the cross, he wasn't just preaching, he was preaching in bad poetry. Hettie collapsed in her seat, the room tilting. It was too much all at once.

"Every page drips with the blood of truth and the wails of righteous suffering. *Ahhh*-men?"

"*Ahhh*-men!"

That *ahhh*-men was it. Hettie had heard enough. She jumped from her seat, kicked aside knees and booted feet and moshing elbows and headed for the door. Above it was a lit up exit sign with a question mark after the word.

"Don't fear the truth!" Pastor Skip shouted from the stage. Hettie could feel the pointed finger at her back, the eyes of the room following her steps. "Eternal life is waiting for all who seek it along the narrow path!"

Hettie had made it just into the hallway when a hand grabbed her shoulder, stopping her with unusual ease. She spun around and found Ruby standing behind her, breathing hard, eyes wild. Could have been the drugs. It was probably Pastor Skip's dynamic stage presence.

"You can't just leave like that," Ruby said. "Do you know how lucky you are to be here? We got you in. You're in now. Don't throw all that away."

"Church? You brought me to a fucking *church*?"

"This isn't a church. We don't *do* churches, Henrietta." The sharp utterance of her full name was such a haughty, mom thing to say. "This is a holy place of worship. A meeting place of the doomed who have been selected for a special message that we'll share with the rest of the world at the proper time."

"What? I don't ... Why did you dress me up like this?"

"Our group is for those who sought meaning in the darkness. Those who don't fit in with other congregations. The dark children. Pastor Skip says—"

"Pastor Skip!" Hettie cried through a laugh that came out sounding something close to insane. She snapped her mouth shut and swallowed her laughter in noisy chunks.

Ruby frowned but continued. "Pastor Skip says we're the special ones. Those who have stared into the abyss and come back, changed and ready for the true eternal."

"Do you hear yourself? Do you—" Hettie had to release another bit of swallowed laughter in disbelief. "And what sort of 'dark child' Christer is a drug fiend?"

Ruby sniffed, mostly out of necessity, but also out of bruised arrogance. "It's necessary for our cover. To move amongst the unclean."

"Bullshit."

Ruby didn't even try arguing, she was so flustered, and wacked to the holy rafters on methamphetamine. "The body is nothing," she shrieked. "It's filth! We contaminate ourselves with every thought, every action."

"Yeah, some actions more than others. You're probably a big time slutbag, too."

Ruby slapped her, shaking now. "I don't share my body with anyone but …" Ruby trailed off, collecting herself. "My sex is not for sale. It's offered up to the Father."

"Yeah, I'll bet it is. With coupons, too." Hettie rubbed the side of her mouth and looked back into the harshly lit basement at Pastor Skip on stage, who was watching them while talking with two frighteningly young girls that reminded her of the goths on the bus.

"What were you doing out at the bookstore?"

"Scouting for people like you. Losers. The worthless. All the lost refuse that is so ignorant and damned."

"Oh shit … It's the Jesus Cult."

Ruby brought back her hand to strike her again.

Hettie held out her chin. "Left side this time, okay? I want to look even."

Ruby stayed her hand, then dropped it quickly. Hettie took one last look around at the freak show that made Barnes & Noble look tame, and pushed past Ruby and out into the hallway.

"Don't leave," Ruby said softly, her voice small, like a little girl's. "I'm sorry."

"You're sorry, all right."

"Hettie … Don't. Leave."

"What?"

"Don't leave alone. You don't know what's out there."

Hettie paused, waiting for an explanation.

"Bad things await for those who reject the light. Forces of reckoning. They do the holy work to those who choose the dark."

Hettie had heard enough and turned to exit. Ruby stopped her again.

"If you leave now, you'll be lost forever. They'll come for you. They'll get you."

"Who?"

"You'll see."

Hettie laughed. Actually laughed, nearly doubling over as she let it all out. All the absurdity and stress and frustrated longing of the last few days and the many months that came before. "Okay, Ruby. Enjoy eternity."

"You too. When you get to hell, look up. I'll be waving down to you."

Hettie laughed again and walked back up the hallway.

XVII.

Hettie sat on the curb several blocks up from the house and the church in the basement and cried. How could she be so stupid? So gullible? She longed for a car to pass by, so she could lay down in front of it. She'd prep the way, and wait for Avery to join her. So incredibly stupid. Waiting. Hoping. Trusting in whispers of a faith that she didn't have. She closed her eyes and began to cry, the tail end of all the laughter that had left her empty.

"You looking for vampires?"

Hettie looked over, squinting through her tears at the two figures that stood back by the fence. She could make out that they were male, vaguely familiar, and smiling. She wiped her eyes, and detected the particular shapes and expensive Victorian styling of Ever and Benthic. *Great*, Hettie thought. *Phase two of the salvation hard sell.*

"No," Hettie said, snuffling and wiping her nose with the ball of her hand. "Not anymore."

"Sure you are," Ever said, smiling his ten-thousand-dollar smile. "You're looking for vampires. You told us."

"I was joking. You guys are a bunch of idiots."

"No, you really are," said Benthic, more laconic than ever, the drugs in his system wearing low. "We can read your mind. Don't you know?"

"Fuck off."

Benthic snarled with what he probably planned to be seduction, exposing the side of his teeth. Sharpened canines were visible. She hadn't noticed them before. "It's not nice to insult a vampire."

"Yeah, well, if I ever run across one, I'll be sure to remember that." Hettie got to her feet and kept her voice extremely calm and measured, stuffing down any waver of what was fighting through her practiced impersonation of a fearless person.

"I got a vampire in my pants," Ever said.

Hettie jerked her gaze to him. His face looked changed. Way too intense. He was breathing hard through his nose, taking in great inhalations of air and whatever scents came with them.

"I do too," Benthic said.

"Yeah, we both got vampires in our pants."

"Batwings and everything."

"I thought you were the nice one," Hettie said to Ever.

"Oh, I am the nice one. Wanna see how nice I can be?"

"Oh, wait 'til you see." Benthic was actually clapping.

Hettie looked down the block at the huge house. No one was outside. Everybody was in the basement, listening to the underground litany sang loud by Pastor Skip. Behind her was nothing. Just mute trees that had seen too much over too much time and an empty city that didn't care enough to watch.

"Yeah, I do." Hettie knew that she was all alone out here with these meatheads dressed up to slum for weird girls. They probably kept photo albums of their conquests. Videos.

The guys looked at each other, half in excitement but also half in shock, as they never expected this answer.

"Come on," Hettie said. "Show me the vampires in your pants." This was a risk, but it was all she had. She knew that it would go from playful to serious work in a matter of seconds. She also knew that she was lucky to know this, so she could prepare herself. Shocked people never move, not until well past too late.

The guys again looked at each other, their bluff called. "You first, dickhead," Benthic said to Ever. Their names were probably Chase and Dillon.

"No you, faggot."

Ever shrugged violently, shoving off some nervous echo. "Fuck this," he said, and reached for Hettie.

She was prepared. She knew what to do, and did it, winding up her leg like a football kicker and letting go the opening kick-off right between his legs. He was moving forward, closing the distance, so she didn't hit him square, but it was close enough, glancing off the upper part of his inner thigh and landing in his pleather-bound crotch. It seemed small, this vampire in his pants, and got smaller still after the kick, whimpering and crawling back into its coffin inside the pelvic cavity. Probably why he didn't actually show it to her.

Ever dropped to his knees. "You *fucking* cunt." He sounded surprised, and drew out the word 'fucking,' for some reason, as if 'cunt' needed a special qualifier.

Benthic grabbed her before she could ready another kick. Kung fu never happened in real life. He laced his finger into her hair and yanked her head back, putting his dry mouth to her ear, wheezing fecal chemical breath. "I'm going to bury you in the fucking ground."

Hettie closed her eyes and tensed her muscles, pushing out her mind to the hospital for an apology while concentrating on turning her body into a living bomb, to charge up every atom and split them all in two, releasing the energy of long dead nebulae that lived inside every bit of stardust that made her. She could do it, she knew. She just had to say the right words. Had to remember. Remember. Push aside the pain of her hair separating from her scalp and remember ...

A whistle, sharp as a gunshot, pierced the air. It wasn't musical, more of a repeated rhythm, like a Morse code of sound.

Benthic jerked his head around, not sure from where the sound originated. Ever was still moaning on the ground. "Shut the fuck up," Benthic whispered to him. Ever didn't.

A man leaned against one of the giant trees. He must have been there the whole time, because he couldn't have walked up on the threesome without being seen by one of them.

"Stop that," he said simply. It was the plain looking man from the minivan. He smoothed out his moustache, either removing bits of food from earlier, or by force of habit.

Benthic sneered at the man. "Stop what?"

The man nodded to Hettie, whose eyes were now certainly open.

"That. Stop that."

Benthic laughed. It wasn't a cruel, villain laugh. Just the laugh of a teenage boy not smart or deep enough to be a villain. He was simply bad. "Who are you, my dad?"

"Certainly not," the man said, shoving his hands into his pockets and walking toward them. "I would have choked you with your own umbilical cord inside the womb." He spoke in a strange, even way, enunciating each word and giving no credence to contractions.

Ever got to his feet on shaky legs. "Move on, old man. This ain't about you."

The man came to a halt in front of them, hands still in his pockets. "Not until he stops that."

"Make us."

The man raised his eyebrows, then shrugged. Before Benthic could start laughing again, the man pulled a small, black length of plastic from his pocket, flicked it once and pointed a now two-foot-long baton at Ever's chest.

"Release her."

"What is this, Rodney King?"

Blue electricity arced from the end of the baton and sunk into Ever's sternum. He went stiff, making a strange, cartoonish choking noise, then collapsed like a brained steer.

Benthic held onto Hettie, moving another hand over her throat.

The man bent down next to Ever and folded his hands over his crotch. He trussed them together with white plastic zip ties, doing the same with their legs, pulling the plastic tight over the thick boots. When he was done, he held out his hand to Benthic, gesturing him forward. "Now you."

"I'm going to kill her."

He waved his hand forward. "Now you. Come."

Benthic measured the situation, weighing the implacable calm of this nondescript man who looked like he belonged in the middle management break room of a low rent insurance firm. Guys like him didn't act the way he did. Reaching his decision, Benthic pushed Hettie at the man and took off up the sidewalk. The man steadied the girl as she came to him, stepped around her and followed the man at a brisk gait, covering a lot of ground with each quick step.

Hettie rubbed absently at her sore face. Both sides hurt now, but only vaguely. She felt drugged. She may have been, considering with whom she had spent the afternoon. A crack and fizzing sound came from the darkness, followed by the impact of wet meat hitting the pavement. Moments later, the man emerged into the lamplight glow dragging Benthic behind him by his pantleg, bound in the exact fashion as Ever.

As the man walked past, he grabbed the pants cuff of the other boy and dragged both down the street to his waiting minivan. He popped the hatch, picked up each, and tossed them inside with surprising ease.

He dusted off his hands and returned to Hettie, who was watching all of this with dim recognition. None of it mattered anymore. He'd probably toss her into the minivan, too. She might even climb in. What was the fucking point of any of it anymore?

The man stood in front of her and shoved his hands back into his pockets. "You need to stop what you are doing, as well."

"What am I doing?"

"This foolish quest of yours. It is not safe, for anyone. Now go home, and forget everything you saw here. I do not feel I have to explain why."

Life began to course through her brain again, her limbs. Her knees buckled, and she sat back on the sidewalk. "I won't stop. I can't."

"You will."

"Never."

The man regarded her, rubbing the collapsible cattle prod against the side of his face. Considering. He stepped forward, and Hettie's heart jumped, but she stood her ground. He put his free hand inside his pocket again. Hettie closed her eyes, building an image of Avery in her mind.

"Open your eyes."

Her eyes opened. The man was holding a business card in front of her face.

"Look at this card."

She did.

"Remember what is written, and go there tomorrow, twenty-five minutes before sundown. Do not be late."

Hettie's eyes grew wide.

"Do you see? Can you remember?"

Hettie nodded slowly.

"Do not be late."

Hettie nodded again.

"Go home."

Hettie didn't. She went to another place instead.

XVIII.

Hettie stood at the bedside. She had never been this close to Avery, in any classroom or locker room or hallway. Not even that day in The Weeds. Each meeting, getting that much closer. There had always been so many people between them. A distance stretched wide by social disconnect. But not anymore. It was just the two of them. One breathing fast. One breathing slowly through the tube stuck down her throat and into her lungs. One sweating into her clothes. One rotting into her bed.

The smell was less strong here, close up. Hettie bent down and sniffed a bald patch of Avery's scalp that stuck out atop the blankets. Her head smelled faintly of Johnson & Johnson baby shampoo, the calling card of a diligent nursing staff tasked with long term patient care. The decay was coming from someplace else. Perhaps from the room itself now, the walls, the air in it, sucking it all out of Avery along with that inscrutable elixir that gave consciousness to a mass of mindless cells. Or maybe Hettie was getting used to it, allowing other things to pop to the surface while the smell of death hovered into the background like a humming motor that the ear no longer hears.

She lifted the blankets and held them up. Avery's body was a collection of brittle sticks shoved inside white nylons veined in blue. Tubes ran in and out of her pale shell, adding and removing while she was slowly erased. A silver cross hung on a simple chain around her neck, resting in the hollow cut by her distended collarbones that pushed up into her skin. Avery didn't look human. She was transformed, like a bird hatchling removed from its shell too soon. Yet she was still transcendent, the girl above all other girls, even above the women, if chardonnay gossip amongst her mother's friends was any indication. In becoming less human, the other parts of what made up the perfect construct of cells that was Avery Valancourt rose to the fore.

Hettie leaned in close to Avery's ear, just as that stupid boy had done in the shadow of those huge trees a few hours earlier. "I found a way," Hettie whispered.

A creak elsewhere in the building caught her attention. High up on the wall near the corner of the room, a hand-lettered sign taped slightly crooked read "NO PHOTOGRAPHY." She hadn't noticed that from the doorway.

"I had faith, and I was rewarded for it," she continued. "Now I'm going to save you. Just hang in there. Hang in there for just a little while longer."

Hettie gently snapped the chain around Avery's neck and removed the cross. Cocking her head to the side like she'd seen couples do in movies, she kissed the side of Avery's mouth, touching her lips to the distended line of cracked purple skin surrounding the respirator.

"Salvation is coming."

XIX.

Hettie sat on the edge of her bed, looking at her room in the morning light like a stranger in a strange land. Even though little had changed in the decor since she was in grade school, she had no connection to any of it now.

She picked up her backpack and left her room, closing the door behind her.

Her parents sat at the kitchen table, eating breakfast. PBS news was blaring from the small TV on the counter.

Hettie stood in the kitchen doorway and took down the string of garlic cloves that always hung on the wall above the light switch. Hearing the rustle of dried out skins, her mother looked up, a small frown bending her lips. Her father glanced over at her, and raised his eyebrows in recognition. "There she is," he said. It was one of those hollow, small talk things he picked up from other men at his work that didn't suit him.

"Didn't hear you come in last night," her mother said.

Hettie didn't leave her spot. She was waiting for them to invite her in, to set a place for her at the breakfast table that was only set for two.

Hettie looked at the garlic in her hand. For a moment, a brief moment, she thought about forgetting the whole thing. The last several months, the years that were waiting for her. It suddenly seemed like a lot. Too much, in fact. She could just melt back into her family unit, attend university, marry the first boy that requests a third date, divorce, watch her children learn to hate her, spend her remaining life with cats and a television set.

All they had to do was ask her. To be her parents and invite her to breakfast as their daughter, not the fully functioning and equally respected human being that lived in the house with them rent-free. Insist that she address them as Mom and Dad or Mother and Father or even Ma and Da instead of their first names, because inside her mind, she never called them by their first names. If they'd only ask her where she had been spending her days, and especially her nights, since she was casually allowed to leave school and any semblance of normal social interactions. Wonder about her. Worry about her. Fear for her safety amid a world that was bred to kill its women. Demand to know why she had taken down a string of garlic from their wall at 8:30 in the morning. Hettie waited for it, dreading but wanting it somewhere deep inside that four-year-old paper doll that lived among the tree rings of her constantly reconstituting form of flesh and bone. She'd do what they asked, if they only asked her.

Her parents turned from her and moved onto the next article, reaching for another slice of bread and moving their conversation to the environmental benefits of switchgrass as a source of renewable biofuel.

If they had looked back, they would have noticed that their daughter was gone.

XX.

Hettie waited just inside the entrance to the cramped backstreet address that was embossed on the man's card. Muelenburg Alley, obviously named for the huge Muelenburg ironwork sign slouching on the top of a red brick factory that made up the right side of the passage, the legs of the M bending in on itself in exhausted surrender. The alley looked as if it would reek of urine and rotting garbage, but it was remarkably clear of refuse of any kind. It looked scrubbed clean, as if prepped for inspection, or the arrival of someone quite special. The red walls were in full shadow as the sun set on what seemed like the other side of the world.

She had changed clothes since leaving her house, and now wore an upscale party dress that was far too expensive and girlie to have come from her own closet. It was from Avery's, and therefore fit her all wrong, clinging and bulging in unfortunate ways. The high heeled shoes were a gorgeously poor fit, as well, causing her to constantly move to relieve the pressure on her blisters, which made finding her balance nearly impossible. If someone— anyone—happened to pass her at that moment, they would have taken her for something far different than what she really was.

But Hettie wasn't concerned with any of that. She was worried that the man wouldn't come, that it was just some sort of setup, and that she wouldn't be able to find her way home, as the public transport services that ran here were spotty at best, and cut off just before sundown. She'd never been to this part of town before, so nothing looked familiar. Nothing stood out as a landmark among the miles of decaying factory buildings that moaned to the modern world through broken window teeth. Standing in this strip of desolate human construction she felt as if she was drifting in forgotten space.

Hettie checked one of her phones, the newest one with the pink rhinestones glued to every available square inch of plastic, and just as the time turned to the new hour, the minivan came into view, driving slow on a street without another parked or moving car in sight. In the dying daylight, she could see that it was an odd shade of light green.

It pulled up to the curb. The man reached back from the driver's seat and opened the side door, which creaked as it slid open on corroded runners. The man looked at her, eyes hidden by the large, plastic frame glasses that had a slight tint to the lenses. He was wearing the same outfit as the night before. She obviously wasn't.

Hettie tossed in her backpack and climbed inside, closing the door behind her. The minivan drove away from the curb.

She rode in the lone bench seat set on the middle track, allowing legroom, and obviously for body room behind her. She smoothed out her dress, then glanced over her shoulder. The threadbare flooring was empty, spotless.

"Where are your passengers from last night?"

"Not here anymore."

Hettie considered this from all angles. She liked the conclusions she reached.

"So where are we going?"

"You will soon see."

Hettie listened to the creak of the car parts underneath her. She had never driven a car before, and rarely rode in them. The experience suddenly seemed exotic.

"You're the Renfield, aren't you?" she stated with a question.

The man said nothing. Hettie looked out the window, not really seeing anything that was out there.

"Are you going to kill me?"

"Me?" The man seemed genuinely perplexed by this question.

Hettie nodded, squeezing the stuffed animal inside her jacket. The thought never occurred to her until after she asked it. The lizard brain had spoken, looking for answers to calm fears of those things outside the reach of the firelight.

"No. I will not kill you."

The way he said it made any follow-up question, or concern about the issue, suddenly seem pointless.

Hettie relaxed a bit, readjusting in her seat. "How did you find me? Like, how did you know to come to that weird fucking church?"

"They knew what you were looking for, so they sent me."

"*They?*"

The man said nothing.

Hettie chuckled a little, her voice sarcastic. "What, the *conclave of vampires?*" She used air quotes, which she immediately regretted, as she hated people who did that.

The man looked at her in the mirror, but offered no reply.

"How could they, though? *Know*, I mean."

"They are very thorough. They like to know who and what is interested in them, and why."

"Do they know why I am?"

"Yes."

"And they've agreed? Agreed to help me?"

"That is to be determined."

"How did *you* find me? Last night."

He gestured with his head. "Those phones you carry around."

Hettie looked into her bag.

"They are very easy to track. You should be aware of that."

"Yeah. I dump them after a time. I guess I haven't lately. Been a little ... distracted."

"Why do you have so many? I see no sense in this."

Hettie squeezed her backpack, now resting on her knees. "Because of what they are, what they tell me. Because of what I can do with them, who I can reach."

"Why do you do this?"

Hettie looked out the window at the passing dead buildings and empty streets. "To ruin their lives."

The man said nothing. Hettie didn't notice either way, as her gaze was focused inward. "I make calls, and I tell whoever picks up all sorts of horrible things." This sounded like a confession, but wasn't. It was a release of a wonderful secret to a person who obviously knew how to keep a few. "I tell them I'm their husband's mistress, or their son's on-call prostitute. I tell the old ones that I'm their granddaughter and then remind them of how grandfather did things to me during bath time when I was three. I call bosses and quit, and order thousands of dollars of merchandise and charge it to a temporary app. I even told one of them that I was calling from the grave."

The man looked at her in the rearview mirror, neither shocked nor amused. Merely curious. "You enjoy this?"

"I do. I really, really do."

"Why?"

"Because people are shit."

The man said nothing.

"Why do you work for them?" Hettie said. "The *They?*" She did the air quotes again. Heaven help her if it was becoming a habit.

"My reasons are my own."

Hettie found his eyes in the mirror. "Maybe someday, I'll steal your phone."

The man returned her gaze. "That would truly be something to see."

The man pulled over and stopped the car. Hettie glanced around out the window, noticing they were on a bridge. She'd never seen this particular bridge before. Not in the city she knew. The man turned around and held out his hand.

Hettie furrowed her brow in confusion. "Is this the place?"

"For those it is."

He gestured again to her pack. Hettie paused. She didn't want to give up her phones, her lifeline to the conversations and text messages and photographs shared between so many people. These were her soap operas, and her bank accounts, and this man wanted to take them from her.

"However this works out," he said, "you will not need them anymore after tonight."

Hettie looked at the side of his face, at those strange, '80s plastic frame glasses. There was nothing to give her a clue as to his intentions with her.

"However this works out," he repeated.

Hettie pulled the seven cell phones of various makes and models and levels of bling and handed them to the man. He opened his window and tossed them out, one by one. Each spun and turned as they dropped from the bridge into the dark river below.

Hettie felt a pang of longing. The man rolled up the window, drove to the end of the bridge, turned around, and headed back across the bridge the way they had come, back into the city. Hettie stretched her neck to get a glimpse of the water as they passed over it, never stopping to consider how stupid it was to expect to see her phones down below. They were long gone by now, pushed out to sea.

XXI.

The sun had nearly set. This would normally be the time for magic hour glow, the weakening rays bringing golds and blues to everything in sight. But out here the dip in light made the buildings seem dark and damp, moldering before the ink of death. If Hettie would have stopped and thought about it, if she wasn't so in her head about what this night meant, she would have properly taken in the panoply of fickle colors, no matter how drab, offered up by a dying day, as it would be the last sunset she'd ever see.

The minivan parked behind a row of RVs, high walled pickups, and transport trucks painted with ten layers of graffiti and cover-up paint. They both got out and walked toward a stout, ten story building that extended deep into the block well beyond view. It could have been wider than it was tall, but it was impossible to tell.

A line of women nearly all the same size turned expectantly at the sound of Hettie's clicking heels, searching eyes locked on the nondescript man and dressed up teenage girl walking past. Their clothing was drab, functional, their shoes sensible. Hettie envied it all, longing for jeans and Chuck Taylors. Pining for socks.

"What are they waiting in line for?" Hettie whispered. Their hungry expressions made her want to hide herself. She couldn't imagine what would bring them in such numbers to this desolate part of town.

"Lottery."

The man walked past the women to the front of the line, and slid back the closed pocket door. The industrial sound of machinery hit her like a punch.

Inside, it was deafening. The air was hot and smelled of cloth and chemicals. Rectangular light banks hung down from the ceiling on thin chains, stripped of light bulbs and wiring, left like upside down tables with their guts removed. Ground-up denim dust filtered through the wide room in a choking fog. The cement floor was stained in swirled patterns from decades of different dyes, coloring the gaudy fashions of outgrown generations. Along each wall, rows of huge steel washers ran golf balls over jeans that would come out perfectly distressed for discriminating buyers in upscale boutiques that could pay to have their clothing broken-in first. The collective racket of the machines sounded like a hailstorm at the end of the world.

Hettie pressed her palms over her ears and tried to squint away the noise. Following the man, she peered into side rooms that snaked off the main at even intervals. In each, a dozen women all the same size, that looked nearly identical behind their respirators, sat hunched over enormous sewing machines. They had the same shaped eyes as the women waiting outside, but were cast down at their work. Stacks of unfinished fabric pieces stacked fifteen feet high loomed next to each woman, like taskmasters watching and counting and waiting for their turn on the table.

She lingered outside one of the side rooms. The man offered his arm and led her onward, walking her into a freight elevator that could accommodate a sedan at the end of the room.

Although Hettie had never been on a freight elevator, she figured it would have directional buttons, but she saw none. The man closed the security cage, the elevator car jerked, then ascended slowly. The bang and roar of the machinery echoed loudly here, worming up the shaft, gaining strength and weird echoes as it rose.

"How can you stand it?" she shouted over the noise.

"You cannot hear it from above," he yelled back.

"It's awful."

"It is necessary."

The elevator continued to shudder and climb, as if the building were hundreds of feet higher than what was visible outside. They passed floor after floor of open spaces populated with thousands of dressing dummies, missing heads and limbs, and devoid of clothing. Nothing moved anywhere in the building above the ground floor. The sound below began to dissipate, but Hettie didn't remove her hands from her ears. It felt safer when she couldn't hear anything, and she was frightened. The source of the fear is what confounded her, and frightened her even more.

XXII.

The elevator came to a stop at the top floor, which was a vast landing that ended at a three-story high white wall with one green door situated in the middle. The sounds from below were completely gone, giving an oppressive immediacy to the new silence. The man pulled open the cage and the gate and gestured curtly for Hettie to disembark onto the open floor that led nowhere else but to the door on the far side of the vaulted room.

"Remember what you said in the car about not killing me, okay?"

"I will not forget."

The man led them across the clean tile floor to the door, locked by two stout slabs of iron. He pulled out twin tiny keys from his wallet, stuck them into offset keyholes and unlocked the slabs. With a simple turn of a knob the door opened and swung inward, letting out the cold, dry air within. The man turned to Hettie, regarding her with a serious face.

"Once you enter here, you cannot leave as you are now. You will depart this place one of two ways, and both of them will be different than anything you have imagined."

"I know," Hettie said.

"I know you know, but are you prepared for this?"

"Is anybody?"

The man regarded her one last time, about to say something, but stopped. The tiny spark of concern in his eyes flickering out. He nodded and bowed to her, gesturing with his hand for her to enter before him. She did, and he followed.

The other side of the wall opened into a massive studio space lit only by wall sconces giving off a low light. The yellowish glow hinted at a beamed ceiling fifty feet high and the width of the entire building. Its length disappeared into unlit darkness, which could have gone on for miles. The air was different in here, as were the dimensions, the way the sound played off the rigid materials, as if they had entered a different place.

The man led her to the center of the room, bowed slightly, turned, and exited, closing the door behind him. Hettie waited for the click of a lock, or the sound of heavy chains, or something menacing like that, but there was nothing.

Hettie stood there for what seemed like minutes. She bent one ankle, then the other, ending up perched atop the sides of her feet. The silence was jarring, the seashell roar of machines echoing in her ears.

"I'm here," she said with a shrug, because she didn't know what else to do. After a wobble, she cursed and stepped out of her heels, dropping down a few inches. She closed her eyes with a sigh of relief.

"Which brings us to the question," a quiet, raspy, almost inflectionless voice came from above her, then finished behind her. "Of why."

She opened her mouth, but found that she needed to swallow. The words she had rehearsed caught in her throat.

"Why—why—why ..." The question framed as a statement fluttered through the air, coming at Hettie from all around her. "Why." The last came from below.

Hettie jumped back, her shoulders hitting something hard that shouldn't be in the middle of a deserted room with her.

"Why do you seek us?" the voice said just inches away.

Hettie spun around, but nothing was behind her. She slowly backed up, stiff legs stumbling over her loose shoes, toes feeling for purchase as she expected the ground to fall away under her feet. She opened her backpack and pulled out the string of garlic cloves, draping it around her neck. Avery's silver cross glittered from its chain wrapped tightly around her fingers. "Are you who I think you are?"

"Why are you bringing attention to us?" the voice sounded above her again. "Unwanted attention." Now next to her left ear.

"That's not want I want."

"Then what is it that you *do* want, girl?"

A figure rose in front of her, as if growing out of the floorboards, a shadow form stretching a dozen feet high. As it stepped forward into the beam of moonlight it shrunk to a more modest seven feet. Hettie sucked in breath as she took in the appearance of what now stood in front of her. It was neither male nor female, but it was human, or at least humanoid. It was unnaturally tall, thin. And naked. Its head was bald and skin sallow but tough, like tanned leather, hanging loose over bones and joints in some areas, and pulled too tight in others. The chest could have supported breasts at some long ago time, but seemed more designed for muscle now than nurturing glands. Where the genitals should have been was just a smudge of hair. It was sexless, this tall thing looming before her, but it seemed to quiver with a sensual anticipation. A lustful fever.

It walked toward Hettie, a slightly mechanical hitch in its step, like a droid, or an expertly guided marionette, one shoulder leading the way, head repositioning itself every few seconds like a fly on a long, graceless neck. Its eyes were near totally black, the sclera peeking around the expanded black irises—or pupils, it was impossible to tell the difference—like a beaten solar eclipse.

"W-What are you?" Hettie said, shocked, fascinated.

The thing's face moved in close to the girl's mouth, watching the shaking play of her tongue behind the teeth, sniffing her breath. "Like nothing you've ever seen before."

It circled her, moving in that jerked, scuttling way that hinted at more bones and joints in its long legs, eyeing the garlic and the cross dangling from Hettie's quavering fist.

It clapped its hands together once, long fingers slapping against each other with a thick, shredded sound. "Are you here to prepare a meal? Perhaps teach us a Sunday school lesson?"

"I'm protecting myself."

"Not with those storybook trinkets."

Hettie looked down at the garlic and the cross. She dropped both to the floor. "I didn't think so."

"Superstitions grow like a virus. Age and retelling does not a fact make."

Hettie put her hands behind her back and lowered her head.

The creature moved in close, sniffing every part of her that could produce a unique scent. "You are frightened. All of you are always frightened."

"No, I'm not."

The thing purred into the side of her head, flicking out its thick, monitor lizard tongue to probe just outside her ear. "You lie."

"I'm just ... surprised," Hettie whispered. "You're not what I expected."

The thing drew back incredibly fast, now standing a dozen feet away. "Oh? You were expecting something else?" It feigned insult, a bruised vanity.

"Yes."

"And what did you think you would find here, girl?"

"I don't know," Hettie said, her mind paging through every vampire image she'd ever seen. She couldn't put into words what she expected, and what she could summon sounded ridiculously cheesy. "Something ... else."

"And what is it that you see now?"

Hettie looked up, fixing her eyes on the figure in front of her. She was finally unafraid. "I see something beautiful."

"*Beautiful?*" The thing laughed, a horrible, raspy sound, like a weeping throat without a voice box. "The flattery of a demagogue in waiting. Do you not have eyes, little tyrant? Should we pluck them out and see for ourselves?"

"I see transformation." She held up her own hands that seemed so basic and ineffectual. Hands that couldn't save Avery. "Evolution."

"Do you see life?"

"No."

The thing's face appeared right in front of Hettie's, startling her, but not scaring her. She wouldn't be scared anymore. "No indeed."

"But I don't want life. Not for me. I want it for someone else."

"Ahhhhh ... A martyr. Saving pennies for a cross."

"No, a savior."

The thing moved back into the shadows, tittering with what was probably supposed to be a laugh, but came out like a choking cough. "But what we give is *not* life. We are made of *disease*, not myth. We do not fly, we do not turn into bats nor smoke nor wolves, we do not bed down with the warm nor sleep inside boxes. We turn into what the directive instructs us to become, making us pariahs of the new, cursed for our age and refusal to join history." The bitterness was thick in its papery voice, filling it with spittle that it spat with each word. "No, what we give, what we *inflict*, is not life. It is an eternal waking death."

"It's better than a sleeping one."

"Is it?"

Hettie nodded.

The creature cocked its long head to the side. "What sort of human are you?"

"What sort of human are *you*?" Hettie countered. Somehow, she had the calm and the confidence of something facing down the end of all things, and welcoming it.

The creature lingered back in the darkness, considering her, the blackness of its eyes so much darker than the room around it that they appeared to be two holes punched into the night. For the first time in what was probably centuries, it was intrigued. Truly curious about the breathing, expectorating sack of blood that stood in front of it, not reeking of fear. To work its brain around something new was exhilarating, and it couldn't help but let out a moan of pleasure.

"You know what we are," it said. "What we are is why you are here."

"You're a vampire."

"We are not."

"You're ... not?"

"No. That which you name does not exist. We most certainly do."

"Then what are you?"

The thing in the darkness grew a bit taller. If it needed to breathe, it would have sucked in a huge breath and puffed out its banded, leathery chest. "We are the First Rulers. We are that which ate the great lizards and those who fell from the sky. We are the invisible, and we are the eternal."

"I don't understand." Hettie was flustered. "I-I think I made a mistake."

"You most certainly did."

The thing emerged from the dimness and loomed in front of Hettie.

"I was looking for a vampire. I was told ... I was led to believe that you were—"

"You *believe*? What do you believe?"

Hettie thought about this, realizing what the thing was asking. "I believe in things that others don't."

"Magic men in the sky? Demons of fire under the ground? What do you believe?"

"I see things. I see things that aren't there, or shouldn't be there, but are. I always have."

The creature's tone changed. "You have the Sight?"

Hettie shrugged. "I have something. That's why I knew I could come here, and that you'd be real and that you'd help me. But I never saw you. Wasn't able to see you."

The figure narrowed its inky black eyes. Sniffed the air. Growled deep inside itself with a sound that was more distracted hum than out of anger.

"You are not like the others. We wanted to see why this was so."

"I hear that a lot."

"I suppose you do."

"But I need to know what *you* are. What you *really* are."

"We will play this game. We have the time."

"But I don't. What are you? You have to say it. I have to hear it. Otherwise everything's for nothing."

"We are that which was here first. We are those that will be here forever."

"That's not a specific answer. I have to go." Hettie turned and walked in the direction she hoped was the door.

"We are what you seek."

Hettie stopped, hope lighting her eyes. "You're a vampire."

"That word means nothing to us. We are the core. We are the root."

"Of what?"

"We are the beginning. You are the end of it. The destroyer."

"But what *are* you?"

"You do not ask. Not yet. We ask. We are growing a chamber that was depleted, but we must be cautious." The thing moved in front of her and posed like a department store mannequin. "What do you see?"

"I see ... a face, but not quite a human face. I see ... bugs. Insects."

It changed its pose, exposing the weird geometry of its structure. "What do you see?"

"Female ... No, male. Neither. Both. I see arms and legs. I see maggots and rot, but I also see ... power."

Its pose and posture changed again, this one more threatening. "What do you see?"

"I see strength, something stronger than death."

"You may ask again."

"What are you?"

The creature melted back into the murk. Hettie could feel it moving around her, sense the way it displaced air without sound, but not without changing the air pressure of the surrounding space.

"Why are you here?" it asked.

Hettie balled her hands into fists. Her impatience was nearly boiling over. "I want to live forever."

"Why do you want this?" The voice sounded bored. It must have heard this for a thousand years.

"Vanity."

"Not enough."

"And revenge."

In the dim light, the creature dropped down from the ceiling far above like a spider cut from a web. It moved toward Hettie very slowly, bringing its face in close, eyes repositioning quickly like a satellite camera, taking in every subtle twitch, blink, and muscle contraction of Hettie's face. It was reading her.

"You lie," the creature said, a ticking sound coming from far back in its throat.

"Not for me. For someone else."

"I know this." The creature's eyes moved slowly over her body, pausing on the points where the blood flowed closest to the skin. The creature knew these areas of the body better than a surgeon. "This is problematic." It disappeared into the darkness again.

Hettie crossed her arms, trying to keep her limbs from shaking from impatience, and a fear that the game might soon be over, and Avery with it.

"Two ... There will be two ..." It seemed to be talking aloud to itself, or communicating with someone else Hettie couldn't see. After a pause, it stood before her, suddenly there when there was only darkness before. "What is to be done with you?" it asked.

"If you won't change me, then you'll have to kill me." These words were not what she meant to say, but she was glad that that part of her that she could never control, nor understand, had taken over and was fully in charge.

The memory of an eyebrow raised under its smooth, mottled forehead.

"I can't leave here alive. I know this. I knew it before I came."

"We do not serve compassion. We serve the needs. The hunger and the survival of the hive."

"I serve the needs, too."

A smile played across the creature's sinewy lips, curling up the right side, exposing a yellowed incisor the length of an index finger. "Very well. But know this, to live forever, one must first die."

"I accept this."

"Death is never pretty, never painless. You will never forget."

"I accept this."

"Tell me your story," it said.

"Tell me yours first."

XXIII.

The man drove the minivan. Hettie was huddled in the back on the floor, pale and shaking, arms wrapped around herself and feet drawn up tight underneath her legs. She pressed her hand against the wound on the inside of her thigh, the spot where the thing from the darkness had opened up her femoral artery and fed like a monstrous hummingbird. It wouldn't give anything of itself to her, only taking from the girl.

The man angled down the rearview mirror. "How do you feel?"

"Like … death," she said through chattering teeth.

The man frowned, unsure is this was sarcasm or irony or just simply a truthful statement. Young people confused him so. All people did, if he was being honest.

"Where are you taking me?" she asked.

"To a proper place. I will show you."

She looked out the window. The first rays of sunlight glowed behind dead buildings. Inside, she could feel herself falling apart, collapsing. She imagined an old black and white movie of washed out buildings falling down around ropes and horses after one of the world wars. "How much time do I have?"

"Not much."

Hettie nodded, then shuddered so violently she moved sideways on the floor. "Can you turn … on the heat, p-please? I'm f-freezing."

"Maybe even less than I thought." He didn't turn on the heat. "There are many things you will learn on your own, but you must be told others before."

She caught the movement of a flock of pigeons that alighted from a hidden roost somewhere inside this graveyard city. They all moved together, without alert or planning. They just knew what the other was going to do, and moved as one organism. Hettie tracked how they moved, and could sense which way they were going to turn before they did a moment later. She would have pointed it out to the man if she hadn't just lost the capacity to speak.

"Find a safe place to die, and make sure it is away from the people and away from the sky."

XXIV.

"They came to me as three boys. Skinny, unwashed, almost feral in appearance, but extremely well behaved. They showed up one morning at the edge of our farm. I saw them from the porch as I was dumping water from breakfast into the flowers planted around the stairs. They stood just beyond our fence, leaning on it, watching us. I sent my boy out to shoo them away, but he came back with them in tow, muttering something about being neighborly, and not leaving a good Christian soul to starve during terrible times.

"The boys were polite. I offered them lunch, but they refused, saying that they didn't want to be beholden to anyone, especially someone like me. I didn't understand what that meant, and asked them to explain themselves, but they didn't say anything. They refused our food and just stood in the yard at the foot of the porch, watching my son and me, taking in the details of the house and outbuildings. After a while, we went inside to set to the inside chores, hoping they'd move on. But they didn't. They stayed where they were, standing in the grass, not talking to each other but nodding once in a while, like they were hearing something we couldn't. The day wore on into the evening, and seeing that they were still out there standing in the yard while we were inside, I became uncomfortable, then agitated, without knowing exactly why. They were just boys, but there was something more to them. Like I could see the men they would become someday. Not exactly men, I reckoned, but something else. Anyway, I couldn't put my finger on it, and even took it for woman worry, but didn't like how it sat inside me. So I went back outside and told them if they weren't going to leave, they could sleep in the loft, above the cows, but had to be gone by morning, as we were going to be visiting relatives the following day. It was a little white lie, but I was raised with manners, you see. That counted for something back then. Considering my invite, they just nodded, each in a different way but all with that same queer smile, and went off to the barn. My son, who was an only child, didn't go with them. This was curious to me. His chores were done, and I'd have laid a pretty good wager that he would want to play some with these boys, as he didn't have anyone else around that was his own age. Just his mother, who didn't like to play much. I asked him if he wanted to go, but he just shook his head, and asked if he could go to bed early. It was like he was sick. I obliged, and turned in early that night myself.

"Hours later, as the night turned in on itself at the midway point, I heard noises on the roof. Light footsteps. Too light for human of any size other than maybe an infant. The noises went up and down the roof. And I heard giggles. Little giggles, like when children are in on a joke that they don't want the adults to know. That the adults wouldn't understand anyway, and kill all of its magic if they did.

"I got up and went to my boy, asking him if he heard the noises too, and he was under his bed, wrapped in his blankets, shaking. I was about to pull him up and out when the sound of the horses screaming took me to the window. The barn was dark. No lamplight or torch. I'd been inside that barn when it was that dark and you couldn't see your hand in front of your face. The horses screamed and screamed, like they were human and understood what was happening to them. Like they knew they couldn't stop it and were afraid of death. After several minutes, the screaming ended. Just like that.

"I grabbed my rifle and sat by the door until daylight. There was no way in hell I was going outside without the sun at my back. After dawn, I waited as long as I could to let the sun remove any shadows between me and the barn.

"They came right before dawn. That must have been as long as they could wait. The door was closed, and then it was open. I didn't see it move. Maybe I dozed off, but I don't think so. The door was open, and the three boys were standing in the doorway. From the stories we all knew, I was certain that if I didn't invite them inside, we'd be safe. The animals outside were gone, dooming us that winter, but at least my son would be safe. My sweet boy, the last of me.

"They stepped inside one by one, moving slowly. I shot at them, squeezing the trigger until the gun was empty. I hit a few, but missed some, too. It didn't matter either way. They took the bullets in like seeds pushed into butter. They fell upon me, stronger than boys that size should be. Stronger than anything I'd ever seen or felt.

"Before they finished me, they brought out my boy, and the bigger one, the older brother, removed the night clothes from his tiny, shaky body. His skin was so white, his ribs sticking out as he breathed hard. The bigger boy moved behind him and wrapped his arms around my child like a backward hug, then he tore open my boy's chest like an overripe peach. That's what it looked like, sounded like. Everything inside him fell out onto the floor, and the two others dug through it, fighting over the liver. No one held me still, but I was frozen. The boy holding my son's dead body like an empty costume stared at me, eyes wide and smile of joy on his face, like he was watching a carnival show. They got to me soon enough, but they did me a different way. They wanted a mother, they said, and I'd be that mother soon enough. Once I joined with them, they said, I'd be part of the tribe. Of the hive. I didn't understand it then, but I do now, just as you will soon, too. And your friend. We'll all be family.

"After they were done, and as I lay dying, I remembered then that I'd invited them in the day before. The invitation was given, even if I'd forgotten. It was only later, far later, that I realized no invitation was needed. They would have come inside anyway."

XXV.

Hettie emerged from the tunnel down by the water just as the sun dropped below the horizon, backpack dangling from one hand. Blood was smeared on her face, the red standing out in sharp contrast to the bone whiteness of her skin, dripping down on the party dress that was soaked grey and dripping black rivulets of filthy water.

The sickness was gone, cured by death. Her heart did not pound, nor did it beat much at all. But she felt alive with fever, consumed by it, a trillion of her new brothers and sisters and fathers and mothers coursing inside her veins, repurposing her genetic code and providing a new form of life that her body did not yet understand.

Her chest heaved like the billows of a forge. Her ribs distended as lungs sucked in huge volumes of air, parsing the information from each new molecule she took inside to a brain that was rewiring itself on a subatomic level, firing up the old passageways to primal instincts humankind had left in the cave. In and out she breathed, her mouth watering. There was so much out there, waiting for her, not knowing she was coming.

She felt ravenous with anticipation, frenzied with the possibility of everything and anything she wished to do. Sounds and sensations bombarded her newly powered receptors, and her parietal lobe exploded with the sensual nectar of hearing and tasting and sensing the physical world stripped raw for the first time, as if the safety plastic had been pulled off and she was finally getting to the real thing. She wanted to tongue kiss the universe. She wanted to eat every living soul on this tiny fucking planet.

And Jesusfuck was she hungry. Starving down to the marrow that was feasting on itself inside her humming bones. She needed to eat something proper, she knew, not tunnel dregs. She needed to eat soon. Had to be strong when she arrived, so she could do what needed to be done without going too far. Without killing Avery. The control could only be achieved if she was suitably trained or properly fed. Hettie was neither.

Running her tongue over her lips, she remembered old, towering trees, a large house and food in the basement. Dancing meat, screaming at a stage. She would go there first. It was on the way. Her family told her so.

XXVI.

Hettie walked, nearly skipped, could have hovered if she was in a movie and not in real life. She was wearing a new outfit that was moderately Victorian and stank of the incense of the basement church, but was clean. Her hair was damp with blood and water, and seemed to find a new style that was thick and unruly and glorious.

She moved down the sidewalk at a brisk pace as her mind uploaded her new reality and her internal processes settled into position. The night teemed with life, and she saw and heard all of it, quickly figuring out what to ignore and what to assess. Every movement around her seemed to whistle through the air, announcing its coming before it arrived. She balanced this with the thoughts and movements from the hive, sent out from across the globe and picked up by her internal antennae that coated every nerve ending. She felt them, what they were doing, and could have mimicked the algorithms of each one moving as it happened, like a flock of birds. Or a swarm of insects. This filled her up with such a profound sense of belonging and connectivity that she felt the urge to weep, which was an act that she somehow knew she wouldn't—couldn't—do ever again.

Familiar smells that came from a near forgotten childhood blossomed in her nostrils. She was near her old neighborhood, and felt the map of each home and place of business open up around her like stepping into a 3D hologram. A limousine passed by, with kids hanging out the sunroof, clutching bottles and each other, howling into the night. They were young and drunk and nothing could stop them from owning the world in just a few short years. They were on the verge.

Up ahead was the hospital. Very few cars were in the emergency parking lot. It wouldn't have mattered if it was filled, like it once was. Hettie was going inside.

XXVII.

Hettie took Avery's hand in hers, holding it up to her chest. She couldn't touch her like this before. With such intimacy and confidence. Now here, and every moment after this, she could. Now she was all hers. She looked at the girl's hand, moving it back and forth like she was examining an artifact. Someone had painted Avery's fingernails. Hettie held them close to her face, and noticed how cracked and flaky the nail beds were. How the cuticles were split. She put Avery's hand into her mouth and rolled the fingers around on her tongue.

Avery didn't move, either not conscious or possibly in a coma. Didn't matter, really. The machines that kept her alive made very few sounds. A slow beep. Her heartbeat. Faintly stirring. Waiting for the end. Hettie smiled at this, and Avery's hand fell out of her mouth and landed limply on the bedding, glistening with Hettie's saliva.

Hettie put her finger in the spittle and traced her wet finger up Avery's forearm, to just inside her elbow, where the catheter was attached to her veins, feeding her drugs and fluids to kill her cells in hopes of keeping her alive. The insane dichotomy of cancer treatment. She cocked her head left and right, trying to take her in from every possible angle.

What are you doing? she heard Avery's voice say, but she obviously couldn't speak through the respirator, even if she was awake. *What are you doing to me?*

"Your blood is killing you."

You don't understand, Avery was trying to say.

"Your blood is killing you," Hettie repeated. "And so are the doctors. I won't let them."

Hettie held up the skeletal left arm. Just below her translucent skin, the partially collapsed brachial artery snaked its way down from the armpit through the center of the arm to the elbow, where it split in two. She removed a syringe from inside her jacket and flicked off the cap. Without taking her eyes off of Avery, she cocked her head to the side and plunged the needle into the carotid artery of her neck. The plunger slowly pulled back, filling the barrel inside with burgundy blood.

Hettie had eaten on the way over, but still didn't trust herself. And her teeth hadn't changed yet. And most importantly, she would have had to tear

Avery open to get to her blood. That wasn't the plan. The needle was the way to go, included in her overnight bag.

When it was full, she removed the needle from her neck, licked clean the needle tip, then inserted it into the IV tubing access port leading into Avery's arm. She let loose the blood inside the syringe, pushing it slowly into the dying girl's veins, mixed into the solution that was her only source of nutrients.

Hettie dropped the bed railing and pulled off the blankets. She removed the respirator from Avery's mouth, carefully wetting the tape and gauze with a damp washcloth brought from the bathroom before pulling it away from her papery skin. She dipped the cloth into a bowl on the bedside table and dribbled water into her open mouth, then washed her face, removing crust from her eyes and pushing wisps of hair back from her forehead, which came loose in her hand. She ran her hand over Avery's head, and what remained of her pageant perfect hair separate from her scalp. Storing these hairs in her jacket pocket, Hettie washed away the scaly build-up on her head like polishing a dusty egg. Avery was now perfect bald, doing an unplanned homage to the colony queen in the tall building.

She then removed each of the sensors and tubes from Avery's fingertips, arms, and her washboard chest. She once thought that these machines were hooked into a central system in the hospital, sending out alerts if there was any drastic change in the readers, but now knew that this was not the case. The shared wisdom of the hive told her so many things. No one would see Avery flatline.

Hettie pulled a party dress from her backpack. It was to match the one she wore, but hers was ruined. Poor planning, as she hadn't accounted for her own time of dying, and where that would be. No matter. She'd dress Avery up and take her someplace safer and cleaner to die. The basement boiler room. Or maybe the morgue. Maybe someplace deeper than that. There were holes in this planet, she now knew.

She carefully ripped the blue hospital gown off of Avery's fragile body, and then gingerly slid her into the dress. She replaced the blankets and laid the stuffed animal, dirty and matted and smelling of sewer, into the crook of Avery's arm, where Hettie's blood had entered her just minutes before.

Smoothing out the blankets, Hettie stood back and waited. The hush of the late hour filled the hospital, allowing Hettie to hear into rooms three floors down, into homes several blocks away. This was her visiting time. It was nearly time for a shift change, and she hoped no overzealous orderly barged into the room. It would be quick and bloody, and it would be a distraction. These next moments were saved for Hettie, and for Avery.

After several minutes, Avery stirred. Her mouth worked over her swollen tongue, then her lashless eyes fluttered. She turned her head slowly to face Hettie, a dreamy expression on her hairless face.

"Wh-whooo ... are ... you?" Avery sounded like she was learning how to speak again. Her voice was dry, raspy, like the queen. It was a comforting sound. Becoming.

"You don't remember?" Hettie asked gently.

"No ... Where ... aaam I?"

"You're with us." Hettie took her hand and caressed it lightly with her fingertips.

"Who?"

"We—" She stopped herself, overcoming her new natural impulse. "*I'm* your friend."

"My ... friend?"

"Oh yes. Your very best friend."

She looked around, blinking, reality—and a tsunami of ancient bacterium—beginning to seep into and eat away the narcotic cloud covering her mind, clearing her up. "Am I dead?"

"Not yet."

"Is this hell?"

"Why do you say that?"

"Because I'm going to end up in hell."

"Why?"

"Because I killed myself."

Hettie didn't expect this. She honestly didn't know what to say.

"I feel really weird," Avery said, voice stronger, lifting her arm to her face, but unable to find it.

"Why do you say that you killed yourself? You got leukemia."

Avery took a deep breath. Several of them, testing out her lungs. She coughed and put her hands to the front of her neck, just above where the respirator had bruised her esophagus. "No ... It only looked like I got cancer .... I need to get up. I feel like I need to get up."

Avery tried to roll her legs off the bed and onto the floor, but she fell, collapsing on the spotless tile. Hettie shot forward and picked her up easily, carefully placing her back on the bed.

"I didn't feel that … Am I in hell?" Avery repeated. "I feel weird."

"You don't remember me?"

"No. Should I?"

"We've been going to the same schools since we were kids."

"And?"

"And, I was probably the last person you talked to on your last day of school."

"I don't remember. Should I remember?"

"I don't know. That's up to you."

"What are you doing here?"

"I'm waiting for you."

"You're what? I don't—" Avery's face changed, her eyes blinked quickly. A flush came to her sunken cheeks, moving her skin from ashen gray to a slurry pink.

"What is it, Avery darling?"

"I don't know … It's … weird."

"I know," Hettie said, dabbing at the sweat that had sprouted up on Avery's hairless brow. "You'll feel weird for a little bit."

"I'm … energized." She raised her skeletal arms above her head, stretching like a waking cat.

"It's the fever."

"Fever?" Avery seemed to panic for a bit, until she remembered where she was, and why she was there. "So, I'm still here. I'm not dead. But a fever …" She stretched a thin smile with cracked lips and exhaled. "Good. Good. Fever will kill me for sure."

"Yes, it will."

"You must be a hater."

Hettie brought a plastic cup of water to Avery's lips. "Absolutely not. I love you."

Avery looked at her as she drank, noticed Hettie's hand stroking her head. She seemed uncomfortable, swallowed the water, then closed her eyes and allowed herself a moment of pleasure.

"What did you mean that it only looked like you had cancer?" Hettie asked.

"I never had it."

"Then why are you dying? *Were* you dying. *Are* you dying? What's killing you, then?"

"I am."

"I don't ..."

"*I'm* killing me."

Hettie's hand stopped, and she withdrew it. Avery settled deeper into her bed, her skeletal frame quivering slightly with the pleasure of memory, fueled by the rising heat of the bacterial infection that was consuming her body a million times faster than she could hope to fight it.

"It was a long game," Avery said, dreamily, "but I was patient. I knew the haters would come for me first, before anyone knew that I was dying. Or why I was sick. I knew it, and they did. Came to pick my bones clean before I was even dead like in those time-lapse videos. But I knew ... I just *knew* that it would all turn around once the diagnosis got out." Avery put on a newscaster's voice. "*'Head cheerleader contracts incurable cancer, school devastated, Mayor cancels Christmas.'* Do you know how rare that sort of PR is?"

Hettie stood up and moved back from Avery, who continued.

"I get to go out on top, in my prime, the eternal celebritante, quitting while she was way ahead."

"What are you talking about?"

"My mom ..." Avery chuckled. "She inspired it all, the genius. The only thing she ever taught me ... Well, aside from how to apply for a credit card. It was breakfast, and she was hungover again. Probably still drunk, and she just broke down at the sink. Told me how much she hated me for being young, and hated herself for hating me for it. And how lucky I was, to be given so much, then how stupid I was for not realizing it. This went on for minutes, and then just stopped. Before she left the room to puke, she said the only thing that made her feel good was that someday I'd know. I'd know what it felt like to lose my looks, lose my man, and lose everything that gave me any sort of worth in this world. Age would come for me, and it would chew me up whole. She said today was the best and last good day of my life, and that everything would go to shit starting tomorrow."

Hettie leaned back against the wall. The buzz of the global hive dimmed in her brain, pushed back by what it was dealing with that lay in front of her.

"That stayed with me. Stayed with me for a *long* time. And finally, it all clicked. *Don't overstay your welcome. Go out on top. Mic drop after your best song*

... So I made my plan, and did my research. I found a poison that exactly mimicked leukemia. They sold it in Russia or Latvia or someplace bullshit like that. I ordered it online, and started taking it in tiny doses. Just enough to do the trick, but not enough to leave a trace. Three weeks later, I was in the hospital, the diagnosis came back, leaked out, and the camera crews arrived."

"Why would you do this? You had everything."

"'*Had*' being the operative word, the monster under the bed, waiting to swallow up '*has*' in one bite." Avery sat up, warming to her confession, feeling more amped up than she had in years. This would be her final interview, her last audience. "Graduation was in two months. Then college, or not. It wouldn't have mattered at that point. Everything I had, everything I built, would have been gone, and the countdown to the end would have started. Shelf life is a motherfucker for us girls, you know? I wanted to go out in my prime. Everyone's a hero when they die too soon, especially the pretty girl. No one remembers the death of an old lady."

"So you did this ..." Hettie had a hard time saying it, as it still hadn't fully sunk in. "*Poisoned* yourself, killed yourself, for ..." She didn't know how to finish.

"Posterity."

Hettie was shocked. She paced the room as she processed it, then stopped and grinned. It was absolutely diabolical. Avery Valancourt was more than she ever could have dreamed. A true soul mate.

Avery shuddered and hacked. "I felt okay for a second, but now ..." She rolled over on her side, away from Hettie. "I don't feel good. I feel sick. Different sick."

Hettie placed a hand on Avery's tiny frame covered in blankets. "You'll be dead soon."

"Yeah, I hope so. You won't tell anyone, will you? At school, I mean?"

"Mum's the word."

Avery closed her eyes. "You can stay here, if you want. 'Til I die."

"Oh, I wouldn't miss it for the world."

"Okay, thanks. What's your name again?"

"I'll tell you later."

"Okay."

They remained like that for a while, until Avery's eyes flew open, bloodshot with fever. She sat up in the bed and looked at Hettie, who was smiling at her with expectation, a parent waiting for their child to find the last Easter egg hidden in the back yard.

"You ... I heard ... You *told* me ... Tell me why you're here."

"I'm saving you."

"I'm not going to die, am I?"

"Yes, you will. Then you'll come back."

"I feel it ... I feel *you* inside me. And others ..."

"Of course you do."

"What have you done to me?"

"I've saved you."

More information was disseminated into Avery from everything that was now inside her. Her eyes flashed with rage. "Bring me a mirror. Now!"

Hettie walked into the bathroom, removed the mirror from the wall and brought it to Avery. She held it in front of the girl lying in the bed. Tears streamed down her face, which contorted with horror.

"Oh my god ...." Her voice was a choked whisper. She slapped at her cheeks, scratched at her hairless head. "I'm hideous."

"You're beautiful."

"How can you say that? I'm a monster! Look at me!"

Hettie set the mirror down. "Someday, we'll look the same, you and me. Like an old married couple."

"You fucking bitch! I know what you're doing. I know what you're doing!"

"You'll never, *ever* grow old. You'll never, *ever* die."

Avery's voice dropped to a whimper. "I'll look like this? Forever?"

"Yes." Hettie couldn't hide her smile. Aside from the tiny hitch with the attempted suicide, everything was working out according to plan. The Sight was pure and true. Just like it always was.

"Where's my nurse. Where's my doctor?"

"They're not coming."

"I'll call the cops. I'll ..." Avery's eyes rolled back into her head. The virus was spreading quickly, finding a foothold, gaining momentum.

"They'll just bury you, and then you'll wake up trapped in a box until the earth blows up a billion years from now. Or, if they figure it out, they'll cut you open to see how you're still walking around without any vital signs."

"What ... did you do to me? This wasn't how ..."

"I told you. I saved you. I brought you back to me, just like you always wanted."

"I don't even know you, you stupid … bi …" Avery was fighting to stay conscious.

"Oh, but you do. You know me better than you know yourself, just like I know you better than I know me. We talked about this all the time."

"You're a fucking … liar. You're fucking … cra …."

"Sorry about that. No hard feelins, huh?" Hettie slung on her backpack. "Come now, you have to go. Before the next shift."

The fever fog cleared momentarily. "Where am I going?"

"You're going to die."

"You said I would never die."

"Yes."

"I don't know what's going on. I'm in hell. I have to be in hell. You're a fucking bitch and I'm in hell."

"No, my love. You're not. You most certainly are not."

Avery's tone changed. She now sounded like a scared little girl, pleading. "I want to die. Why can't I die?"

"All in due time."

A shudder wracked Avery's emaciated body. The fever was deepening, sinking in its trillion tiny teeth. She lost consciousness. The strain and shock and infection was too much after what she'd been through. Hettie bent down and lifted Avery from the bed, the expensive blanket and layers of hospital bedding falling away onto the floor. She carried her toward the door like a little girl toting a dolly.

"Who … are you?" Avery's eyes drooped open, she pawed at Hettie's face. "I'm your family. Your BFF."

Avery smiled a horrifying smile, blood soaking between her teeth. "BFF," she croaked. "I don't … feel … right." Her voice didn't sound right, either.

"You won't for a while, then you will."

"Promise?" Avery vomited blood on Hettie's shirt. No worries. She had a spare stowed in the backpack. Lots of room for lots of things in that backpack.

"Would we lie to you?"

They emerged into the hallway. A phone rang over and over again in an empty security kiosk. Every ten feet or so, there was a lump of something human, covered in blue or white fabric, splashed with blood. Thick red streaks led from the hall to side rooms with shut doors and no lights on inside. The morning crew would be arriving soon. No time to waste.

The girl and her swaddled bundle moved down the hall and stopped in front of the elevator at the far end of the corridor. Holding Avery easily with one hand, Hettie pressed the down arrow button with the other.

Avery looked up into Hettie's face like a newborn, the last of her energy draining from her slackened mouth and swollen tongue that were giving up their primary functions. "What're... we doing?"

"We're leaving."

"Why?"

"Because you don't need to be here anymore."

"Going home?" There was that winning smile again, becoming more ghastly by the second.

"No, we're not."

The elevator dinged, and the doors slid open. Hettie carried Avery inside the elevator car and pressed the lowest button labeled M.

"Where're we going?"

"Up," Hettie said. "We're going up."

ALSO FROM THIS IS HORROR

Lightning Source UK Ltd.
Milton Keynes UK
UKOW05f1811010317
295675UK00024B/660/P